THE TURNING BLADE

THE TURNING BLADE

Clare Frances Holmes

Chivers Press　•　G.K. Hall & Co.
Bath, Avon, England　　Thorndike, Maine USA

ESSEX COUNTY LIBRARY

This Large Print edition is published by Chivers Press, England, and by G.K. Hall & Co., USA.

Published in 1996 in the U.K. by arrangement with the author.

Published in 1996 in the U.S. by arrangement with Laurence Pollinger, Ltd.

U.K. Hardcover ISBN 0–7451–3990–6 (Chivers Large Print)
U.K. Softcover ISBN 0–7451–3994–9 (Camden Large Print)
U.S. Softcover ISBN 0–7838–1624–3 (Nightingale Collection Edition)

Copyright © Clare Frances Holmes 1983

All rights reserved.

The text of this Large Print edition is unabridged.
Other aspects of the book may vary from the original edition.

Set in 16 pt. New Times Roman.

Printed in Great Britain on acid-free paper.

British Library Cataloguing in Publication Data available

Library of Congress Cataloging-in-Publication Data

Holmes, Clare Frances.
    The turning blade / Clare Frances Holmes.
      p.   cm.
    ISBN 0–7838–1624–3 (lg. print : lsc)
    1. Large type books.   I. Title.
[PR6068.O45359T87   1996]
823'.914—dc20   95–49323

THE TURNING BLADE

THE TURNING BLADE

CHAPTER ONE

Life was very quiet in Pomfret Magna. Here, in deepest Somerset, time seemed to stand still, or at least to have the beat of a bygone age. Around us the fields stretched, and the hills; trees and flowers seemed to grow slowly, as if reluctant to come alive.

The year was 1813, and I was sixteen. I lived with my Aunt Rebecca in the village. She was the widow of a clergyman with a small annuity of her own. It was enough for the two of us; we did not want, but there was nothing to spare.

Yet we would not have known what to do with idle luxury, for our days were a mêlée of effort and activity. After the usual chores we did needlework, played the harpsichord or the flute, went to church, made preserves, and cured hams. I cannot understand the impression I had of total inactivity; of being like a vessel becalmed; or like a spirit who had not found a home.

My aunt was in advance of the times, for she insisted that I should receive an adequate education. Mr Hubbard, the curate, was my mentor; and under his tuition I learned French and Latin, and how to conjugate irregular verbs. Yet still I could not understand why I was filled with the certainty that there was more to life, than this. Whichever way I looked, Pomfret Magna and its inhabitants seemed to offer nothing to my questing spirit.

At this time, I remember, I was tall and slim; my hair was of chestnut hue, and it fell in natural ringlets upon my shoulders. My colouring worried me a little, for it was of the uniform shade of perpetual sunburn; my skin was like honey fresh from the comb, and my lips, though generous, seemed unmarked. I thought that Fate had played some trick upon me, that I had no flush of colour to warm my countenance; and my eyes were hazel flecked with green—another mark of the unusual in my appearance.

Aunt Rebecca was short and stout, and wore a great many hand-embroidered garments. She was usually festooned with home-knitted shawls, and her dresses were trimmed with smocking. 'If you pinch your cheeks each night, Felicity,' she said to me, 'really hard, and bite your lips, perhaps the colour you lack may be induced to enliven your skin.' But in spite of repeated slaps, my cheeks remained the same, and my lips did not blossom into a crimson Cupid's bow. No wonder I felt some depression about my appearance; and indeed about the whole circumstances of my life.

My aunt was very concerned about finding me a husband, and one day when she returned late from church she said, 'Mr Hubbard asked to see me, after matins, Felicity. He took me into the vicarage and told me ... yes, he wishes to court you. He asked my permission to deepen your friendship with a view to making you his wife!

'Are you pleased, dear child? This solves so many problems for you. Don't think I don't know that your life is dull and uneventful, and that young companions are scarce or not to your taste. But to be a vicar's wife, and have your own establishment, and your own family—why, your unsettled feelings would soon diminish, and you would find a new interest and involvement with life.'

I did not need to ponder the matter. My mind was quite made up. Mr Hubbard was quite old in my view, almost thirty. He was tall and angular, and his rather raw, crimson colouring seemed incongruous to my eyes.

'But Aunt Rebecca, I could never marry Mr Hubbard,' I replied. 'Such a thing is out of the question. I like him, and respect him as a vicar and a tutor. But anything more is impossible. No, please do not try to persuade me, or mention this again.'

I know that my aunt was disappointed. She said rather crossly, 'So you will be an old maid, then. You will be on the shelf at eighteen, and no one will look at you. I have done my best for you, Felicity. I really cannot fathom you at all.'

'Please tell me about my mother, Aunt Rebecca,' I said, to take her mind off her disappointment, and this was a tale I loved to hear. My mother had been young, beautiful, elegant, gifted. But when I was a small child she had been killed in an accident to a coach. Both she and my father had died at the same time.

My Aunt Rebecca did not dwell on the accident, but upon the grace and charm of my mother, who filled my mind's eye with a kind of comfort and benison. The aura of her personality seemed like distant perfume; the warmth of her memory shed what glow there was over my rather barren days.

'But her sister Diane, now. She was a different person altogether,' Aunt Rebecca said.

'She was rather like your mother in appearance, yet their personalities were so different, their aims in life far from the same.

'Diane lived here in Pomfret Magna, in this very house with the gabled roofs, in her younger days. Then, when she was in her teens she went on a visit to London, to stay with a relation of your late uncle's. And there, an unexpected circumstance developed in her life. She met a titled gentleman named Sir Toby Bullough.

'Sir Toby was visiting my husband's cousin, and he took wine with the family, and of course, met Diane. Sir Toby was not married, though he was no longer young. He was greatly taken with your Aunt Diane, and asked leave to call to see her again. Well, to cut the matter short, within a short time he proposed, Diane accepted his proposition, and within a matter of weeks, she became his wife.

'They live now in Richmond, where I understand they have a very fine house. I have never seen it,' Aunt Rebecca said, and clearly this neglect on the part of Diane caused her regret and pain. 'But I understand her days are filled to overflowing, for they have become attached to the court of the Prince Regent, and take part in many, if not all of the Prince's entertainments and his social life.

'Mr Hubbard does not approve of the Prince's activities, and nor do many of his subjects,' my aunt resumed. 'The Prince should be paying more attention to the war which is raging on the continent against the dastardly French and Portuguese, and occupying himself with the defence of this country.'

'But surely the Duke of Wellington has triumphed in Salamanca,' I replied. 'Mr Hubbard told me of this, and that the campaign in the Pyrenees must be almost over. Surely the danger to our country is considerably lessened, now?'

'Do not you believe this for one moment,' my aunt replied. 'Napoleon is far from finished, and is all set to pounce upon this country as a cat upon a mouse.'

'But I cannot believe that the Duke of Wellington will allow him to get to grips with our country,' I answered. 'And surely the king himself will have some say.'

'The king is ill, some say mad, and his

counsellors are not to be relied on. And just look at the state of affairs in this country. Unemployment. Rising prices. Social unrest. Truly!

'Please go to the kitchen and put the kettle on the hob to brew us two cups of camomile tea, Felicity. Indeed, just to mention Napoleon's name and these troubles has an unsettling effect upon me, and disturbs my digestion and my mind.'

And so life continued in this way for another year. The summers seemed long and hot; the sun shone from a cloudless cupola of blue. And during the winter the rain fell gently, and the snow blanketed the landscape and our tiny village and community, submerging us with anonymity and holding us in thrall amid frost and ice.

And then, in the early Spring of 1814, when I was seventeen, an unusual event occurred. A letter from my Aunt Diane Bullough arrived for my Aunt Rebecca, at our house, The Crested Gables, in Pomfret Magna.

Aunt Rebecca tore the epistle open with trembling hands. She had to sit down beside the wood fire which burned day and night in our retiring-room, so great was her perturbation. After some time she motioned to me to come to her side.

'Pleased be seated, Felicity,' she said, 'for I have some intelligence for you. Listen dear child, and I will read to you what your aunt has written.

'My dear Rebecca,' my Aunt Diane wrote. 'It is so long since I heard from you, and I trust that you and Felicity are in good health and spirits. Both Sir Toby and I are enduring without complaint the ardours of life in London—so different from life in Pomfret Magna, I assure you! I have recently had the honour to be received by Queen Charlotte, and His Majesty asked me to take a glass of punch at a recent reception! But of course I do not forget life in Pomfret Magna, or that my only surviving relatives dwell there still, and make that enchanting village their home.

'To speak frankly, Rebecca, though Sir Toby and I enjoy a felicitous married life, and long constantly for a family of our own, so far our longings have been unfulfilled.

'Which circumstance has made me think frequently now of Felicity, my niece, and a young girl I have not seen since she was a child, when she entered your care upon the death of her mother, Annabella.

'They say that blood is thicker than water, and believe me, that is correct. For I feel I would dearly love to see Felicity again, and I am writing to ask you, dear Rebecca, if you will allow her to come and visit Sir Toby and myself at our residence near to Richmond Park?

'We will do all we can to give her a period of enjoyment and relaxation. There is much of historical interest in London, and many works of art on view. You could regard it as a finish to her education! And to myself and Sir Toby, it would give great pleasure to entertain our young relative, and we would do all in our power to give her happiness, and add to the tenor of her young life.'

Denials trembled upon my aunt's lips. The perils of life in London, the dangers of the journey to the capital, the unaccustomed events which must face an unschooled visitor to Richmond... All were visible upon her face and in the shadowing of her blue eyes. Then she halted her expected denunciations, and placed her hand upon my arm.

'The decision shall be yours, Felicity,' she said, with quiet intensity, and her own warm and confiding smile. 'Go to your room, and think the matter over, and then tell me your decision. The conclusion must be yours, and yours alone.'

I knew in that moment that my aunt was fully aware of my inner striving, and my secret longings. I went to my room underneath the crested gables, and looked out over the landscape before me. Gazed at the bushes trembling into greenery; and the wayside flowers reluctantly emerging from obscurity into life.

I longed to experience every facet of human life. Whatever living had in store for human beings, that is what I yearned and craved to experience with all my mind, my spirit, and throughout the whole of my body.

I did not desire to excel in the arts or scholarship; I did not wish for the adulation following valiant deeds. I yearned only to feel, to know, to draw into my consciousness all the emotions of all the occasions and events of human life.

Love, passion, birth, death, marriage, I longed to know their nature and feel their consequences. The heights and the lows; the supreme and the futile; the tragic and the humorous. Whatever life could hurl at me, that is what I longed to taste, to perceive, to realize, to experience.

I turned from the placid landscape of the village and ran down the worn oak stairs. I told my Aunt Rebecca my decision, and as I clasped her in my arms and poured out my thanks to her for her goodness to me, I know that tears poured down my face, and sobs racked my body.

She quieted me as if I had an illness, and when my weeping was past, I saw tears stand in her own eyes. But she bade me prepare my clothes for the journey, and she herself sat down and began to compose a reply to Lady Diane Bullough, at her house near Richmond Park.

Mr Hubbard himself took the epistle to the inn to meet the mail-coach. And so the die was cast. The decision was taken; the way chosen. But none of us could foresee where this course would lead; or the events upon the way which would engulf us all.

CHAPTER TWO

The mail-coach drew up at its appointed destination. This was a junction known as Gallows Greens, on the outskirts of the capital. There I found a carriage waiting for me. A maid stood beside the door of the vehicle; she greeted me civilly, and said:

'Welcome to London, Miss Felicity. I am Bloomingfield, Lady Diane's maid. She bade me to meet you, and accompany you to Rivermead House, her home in Richmond. Please to enter the carriage. I will attend to your valise.'

So saying, this tall and rather rawboned woman, with iron grey hair and dark eyes, saw me into the conveyance. She handled my rather heavy leather case as if it was as light as air. I tried to engage her in a little conversation as the carriage sped through the purlieus of London, skirting the River Thames as it did so. It was spring now, and many of the wayside trees and plants were touched with green.

I was unprepared for the size of my aunt's house, and the grounds which encircled it. This domicile sat on the top of a small hill, surrounded by greenery and rather mazelike walks. Clearly it was of Queen Anne design; and authentic, there was no doubt of that. A sense of alarm assailed me, and I wondered if I should be able to acquit myself well, if the milieu was to be formal, and rather grand in style.

The carriage drew up at the foot of steep stone steps, and Bloomingfield and I began to climb upward to the front door. Inside the hall, I gasped with astonishment, for I had never seen such magnificence before.

The floor was tiled with Italian marble, and the walls were panelled with dark woods. Oil paintings hung upon the walls, and statues in armour seemed to stand in every corner, like invisible guardians of the scene. Then a faint sound made me lift my head, and I saw who was clearly my Aunt Diane descending towards me down the stairs.

I did not know that anyone dressed like this for everyday occasions. At home in Pomfret Magna, we wore worsted and cottons for our daily chores. Velvets and silks were reserved for best, and were stored carefully between lavender-scented sheets until again required.

But Lady Diane wore a dress of maroon velvet trimmed with lace at the throat and down the sleeves. Her dress had panniers too, and her feet I could see were shod in finest kid. Jewels winked at her ears and throat. I felt suddenly *gauche*, out of place, and quite unequal to my relation and the circumstances in which she lived.

I saw her eyes sweep over me, as she finally came to meet me. Was there a sensation of relief in her glance, as she scrutinized me so closely, without at all appearing to do so?

Then a smile lit her face and was reflected in her fine, brilliant blue eyes. Her features were rather aquiline, but her face was beautifully shaped. Her hair was dark and framed her face with curving shadows. She must have been well over thirty; but she was clearly still a woman at the height of her attraction.

And then I felt her embrace. 'Dear Felicity! What happiness to see you at last! I have thought of you often, but circumstances have not allowed me to get in touch with you. And your mother! She dwells always in my mind. And you resemble her. You have her gracefulness and charm, and your unusual colouring is hers too. Come. Let us take a glass of wine together, and then Bloomingfield will take you upstairs to your room, and help you to unpack.'

We entered what was clearly the salon, a large room furnished again in Italianate style. I was later to discover that Sir Toby's father, from whom he had inherited the property and its contents, had been in thrall to Italy, and had honoured that country by copying its furnishings. But now, I did not consider this. The wine warmed me, and my aunt's attentions eased my uncertainties and doubts. She asked me many questions of Aunt Rebecca and our life. Then finally, she indicated that I should retire to my room.

I found that my private room was at the back of the house, and looked over the rear gardens, which sloped downward to a river. Surely, this was the Thames? Again the room was elaborately furnished, and elegantly arranged. The invaluable Bloomingfield had already put away my clothes, and had laid out a dress suitable to wear for the evening dinner.

She told me that this was taken early, at six o'clock. For afterwards my host and hostess often attended evening receptions and levées, where a later supper was taken. I gathered that there was much conviviality at these affairs, though this was not stated by Bloomingfield; and I guessed she had a sour, rather disapproving disposition.

When I entered the salon at nearly six o'clock, I found that my aunt was already seated there, taking a glass of wine with her husband, Sir Toby Bullough.

Sir Toby rose when I entered, and approached me in an amiable and courteous way. I saw that he was of medium height, rather stout in build, with hair of an auburn hue. His colour was fresh and pleasing; his eyes brown, with sandy lashes. He was clearly considerably older than Lady Diane; but his voice was resonant and pleasing in timbre. I liked him on sight, and hoped desperately that he would like me in return.

I remember little of this evening meal and the conversation, for I suddenly became very tired, and exhausted by the impressions which had assailed me. Both my host and hostess seemed to realize this, and after the meal, they bade me retire to my room. My aunt offered her cheek to be kissed; and Sir Toby held my hand. I felt heartened and encouraged by their kindness and concern.

Accidentally, I left the door of the salon ajar. As I began to cross the hall, Sir Toby's voice came to my ears quite distinctly. I stood quite still as Sir Toby mentioned my name.

'She is a pleasant child, Diane, and I would not wish her harmed. I do not know what is your purpose in bringing her here, but I know it cannot be to her advantage. Yet I beg you not to embroil her in your machinations. Do not make her a party to one of your plots, so that her innocence is smirched, and her life lies around her in ruins.

'I like her very well, I could not bear adverse events to harm her. Let her go, Diane. Do not involve her in your ploys, this time.

'Have you not thought that the misfortunes you create for others, may one day rebound upon yourself? You have escaped immune so far. But it would displease me greatly if this young girl, Felicity Lowe, was harmed in any way. I could not bear to see her ruin or disgrace.'

* * *

The next day a dressmaker arrived with her dolls. We inspected the styles and fabrics, and my Aunt Diane made her choice.

'But of course you must have an entire new wardrobe,' she said. 'It will be my pleasure to provide this. Regard it as a gift from a favourite aunt to a beloved niece! See, this apricot silk will become you well. You are not old enough for aigrettes, but pleated lace and embroidered silks will be fitting for decoration.

'Madame Jasper! How soon can you have these garments completed? Two weeks? But come. London is full of willing seamstresses. And this dress of mine, unworn, I beg you to alter today. Miss Felicity and I will attend a levée this evening, and she must make a favourable impression. To be suitably dressed adds to the pleasure of the occasion,' my aunt informed me. 'You will find this out, dear child, now that you are about to sample the social life of the capital.'

And so I was measured, prodded, corsets were laced upon my body, garters tightened, my feet forced into narrow pumps. But my aunt was pleased with our progress, and when, later that day, I stood before the mirror of my room ready for the evening occasion, she gave me a token of her esteem.

'Take this bracelet, dear Felicity. It was your mother's. I wish you to have it. You will do me credit, my dear. I am more than gratified by the way you have turned out.'

She looked at me in a measured way, her eyes half closed, her lips in a narrow line. The thought came to me that she had taken, to her satisfaction, some step in a private plan brewing within the secret places of her mind.

'No, there can be no evening meal for you,' she said as we went down the stairs. 'Food flushes the skin and distends the body. You will have refreshments at Lady Effingham's house. She is a mean creature, but her cold table is celebrated. Sit in the salon while Sir Toby and I have a small repast.'

My Aunt Diane was elegantly dressed again in velvet of a deep blue shade, which seemed to highlight the midnight sheen of her hair. Her jewels were many and set in filigree gold. I caught Sir Toby's eyes upon her, and clearly he admired her appearance, and her social poise and aura of fashion and authority. The thought came to me that he was proud to have her by his side.

Before we set off, indeed, in the very hallway of Rivermead House, my aunt drew me to one side.

'I must inform you, dear Felicity, of what you may not be aware. In London, and especially in circles attached to the court, manners and morals are not as they are elsewhere. And certainly not as they were in Pomfret Magna.

'For instance, I do not know whether the Prince Regent will attend this soirée this evening or not. He is, as perhaps you know, closely attached to Mrs Fitzherbert, and in truth, many say that they are secretly married, and she is already his legal wife.

'But at the same time, the Prince pursues other ladies. And Lady Effingham is one of these. Indeed, it is said that she gives her favours freely to the Prince, hoping to displace Mrs Fitzherbert from his favour and his life.

'But the Prince is a wily lover. He keeps several ladies in a state of suspended animation. Like a Flanders conjurer my dear, with a handful of coloured balls! I mention this only so that you will be aware of the situation. When one knows the inner secrets of a situation, one does not make gaffes. And to make a gaffe is the worse thing that can happen to one, in this society, my dear.'

Sir Toby had appeared to catch the last part of his wife's discourse to me. He added, 'You are giving her the wrong impression of our circle, Diane.' He turned to me. 'There are many people of integrity and honour in our sphere. Not all are cuckolds or deceivers. You will sift the wheat from the chaff in time, Felicity. But unfortunately, the sifting takes a little while.'

I had a great deal to think about as I drew my velvet cloak about me, and we prepared to go down the steps to the carriage which awaited us. But Sir Toby's words and concern for me warmed and comforted me. I felt I had an ally within the household, and one I could trust. For I had begun to feel threatened, and that I was entering a sphere which was alien to me; and where events awaited me which I could not foresee. And with which I should be greatly taxed to encompass, or overcome.

* * *

I would love to be able to record in detail my impressions of the reception at Lady Effingham's house. That this was a brilliant and privileged gathering was evident, yet so much seemed to occur, that all but the general pattern was blotted out of my mind. I can recall only the kaleidoscope of colour; the vivid lights of the crystal chandeliers; the contrasts of the uniforms of the men; the sumptuous fabrics and elegant style of the women's dresses: the sparkle of precious stones, the sound of the violins, the high-pitched tone of constant badinage and conversation; the fumes of cigars, perfume, and the aroma of freshly poured wine.

It soon became apparent to me that my Aunt Diane knew almost everyone present; everyone of consequence, that is, for I had early realized that my relation wished to know only those of high degree. She had little use for those of lesser station—unless, the unbidden thought came to my mind—they could aid her in the execution of her hidden and secret plans.

But she was greeted with acclaim by all whom she honoured with her attention. And she was scrupulous to present me, in amiable and glowing terms, to all she acknowledged. I appreciated this, for I felt hopelessly lost in this concourse; and indeed, I felt that without my aunt's commanding presence by my side, I would have turned and fled the room and the gathering; and would have hidden myself in the shrubbery, or in the darkness of the London night, outside.

It was towards the end of the evening that a man entered the room, alone. He was dressed in the evening clothes of the time, yet there seemed about him a touch of discipline, an erectness of carriage and formality of bearing that might mark him as a soldier, or one used to military matters. He paused on the threshold of the room, and surveyed the scene before him. He was unhurried, and I gained the impression that there was nothing of which he was afraid.

In the brief moments of my first sight of this man, I observed that he was around thirty years old. Tall and lithesome in build; yet there was also something stalwart about his shoulders and arms. His hair was fair, touched at the roots with auburn; his eyes grey, his colouring fresh yet not florid. His gaze was calculating, as if he had all the situations of his life well in command.

'Why, Anthony!' I heard someone exclaim. 'We are all waiting for the Prince Regent to enter, but instead of his Royal Highness, here you are! Come, take wine. A quadrille is about to begin. Join the throng. I believe Diane is nearby. Yes, there she is, with the pretty young miss from the country, her niece.' And so saying, the unknown guest gestured with his arm in the direction of Diane and myself. I saw then that the newcomer was beginning to make his way towards us.

I had blushed crimson at the unexpected remarks which had drawn attention to myself, in the midst of this sophisticated throng. I glanced at my Aunt Diane to see her reactions to this comment; and the expression upon her face astounded me.

The blood had coursed through her face and neck at the sight of the unknown man. Her eyes shone as she regarded him; her hands shook; it seemed that the whole of her body trembled. Then she had hidden her consternation behind her oriental fan. And when the gentleman in question stood before us and bowed, she had gained control of herself. She was pleasant though formal; her attitude was that of a social friend.

She effected the introduction. 'May I present Lord Anthony Lycett, an honoured acquaintance of my husband Toby and myself. Anthony, please to meet Miss Felicity Lowe, my niece, who is staying as a guest in our home.' She led the conversation skilfully for a moment, indicating to Lord Anthony and myself areas of mutual interest, and concern.

Lord Anthony listened attentively, but without effusion or expressions of pleasure. As soon as this interview is over, he will leave us, never to return, I told myself. The thought disturbed me. I longed to have something brilliant to say to hold him by my side.

'Please pardon me,' my Aunt Diane was saying. 'Lady Effingham has beckoned to me, and of course I must attend her.

'Anthony, please take Felicity into the supper-room and see that she is served from the cold table. She has had scarcely any wine, either. We have been remiss. We have not fostered that spirit of gaiety which the Prince himself loves.'

With kindly smiles upon both of us, my Aunt Diane withdrew. Lord Anthony Lycett and I were left alone—though in the centre of a boiling cauldron of movement and gaiety—and carefully we looked at one another.

I was unprepared for the scrutiny of his eyes. He looked at me as if I was or could be of importance to him. He looked at me as if he was comparing me with some image in his mind.

As for myself, I had never seen a man like Anthony Lycett before. His good looks, his air of authority and competence, his social presence, the sense of a deep and complex personality, affected me profoundly. I know I was trembling as he offered me his arm.

I stumbled a little as we began to pass through the heaving throng. I felt his arm tighten on mine, as if to give me his instant support. He turned and smiled at me, and it was as if all the uncertainties of my nature were revealed to his eyes. He steered us surely from the crowds into the comparative quietude of the supper-room.

By this time I was ravenously hungry, and in spite of my aunt's instructions concerning food, I began to enjoy the sumptuous viands laid out before us. Lord Anthony seemed to find pleasure in my uninhibited enjoyment of the food; but his pleasure was kindly and without criticism or malice, and soon I too was laughing, as we finally found a chaise, and sat down side by side.

I shall always remember my first conversation with Anthony Lycett. He turned upon me the full force of his attention. I was the focus of his interest and his enquiring mind.

He asked me about myself; my pursuits; my interests, things I cared for. He questioned me about my life with Aunt Rebecca in Pomfret Magna. I told him about Mr Hubbard, and the long uneventful days; the lessons in French and Latin; the hours spent in sewing and the making of preserves.

He asked me about my mother and my

father; and what I remembered of those early days. He listened with attention to all I said in reply.

Yes, I opened my heart to Anthony Lycett. For this was the type of conversation I had already missed in Richmond. There, at Rivermead House, all attention was on appearances, fashion, privilege, the attainment of material gain. But here and now, with this handsome and sympathetic man, I felt I had met a kindred soul who cared also for the imponderables of life. My yearnings and the secret wishes of my heart were all laid before him. It was a relief to speak, I felt, to someone whose inner nature matched my own, and who would understand.

Within a short space of time, my Aunt Diane appeared, and with her was Lady Effingham, to whom I was presented, and to whom I curtseyed in the accepted way. 'The Prince has not been able to attend this evening,' she said. She tried to hide her disappointment. 'He has sent his apologies. Matters of state have detained him. Lord Castlereagh, the Prime Minister, wished to have an audience about this accursed war with the French. And so, of course, the Prince had no choice but to put matters of diplomacy first.'

When she had gone, my Aunt Diane said, 'I imagine that Lord Castlereagh wears a dress and wraps his hair in a silken turban. Yes, it is Mrs Fitzherbert's turn, tonight.'

Then she turned to Lord Anthony. 'Would you care to return with Toby and myself to Rivermead House, there to take a nightcap? Toby particularly would be honoured by your presence. He has said only recently it is an age since he saw you.' She laid her hand lightly on Lord Anthony's arm.

In the salon of Rivermead House, the conversation was at once general, and Sir Toby was indeed delighted to converse with Lord Anthony again.

'You have been absent from the social scene for a time,' Sir Toby chided Lord Anthony. 'You tell no one where you go. But you young unattached bachelors have your own secrets and designs. *Cherchez la femme*, no doubt. Felicity, you are pale. Would you like to retire?'

I acceded to this suggestion, wishing to grant my hosts privacy, and I felt I had much to ponder in my own mind. I bade farewell to my relations and their guest. I must have bored him, I thought, as I curtseyed to Lord Anthony. No doubt he will never wish to see me again.

Later that night, when I had taken off my intricate dress and underclothing, and had put on my shift, I heard a sound from the hall below.

Suddenly, I had an intense longing to see Anthony Lycett again. It was as if my life depended upon it. I yearned to see his face and form once more.

I opened the door of my room carefully, and stepped out onto the landing. Below me the hall stood empty, except for two figures close to the front-door.

My aunt and Lord Anthony Lycett stood together, deep in conversation. Softly, though clearly, my aunt's words came to me: 'So you have met her, Anthony. What is your opinion? Will you not congratulate me that I have come up with the perfect specimen, the ideal subject for the purpose in question?'

Anthony Lycett was deep in thought. 'I could congratulate you, because you have done well. But she is not a tame pigeon, or one easy to deceive.

'She is young both in body and experience. She longs to encounter life, and impose her own terms upon all that life can bring against her. And when she does this ... She will be formidable. I would not like to be the one to try to break her, when she is mature.'

'Stuff and fiddlesticks,' replied my Aunt Diane. 'The present is the time. Now is the necessity and now is the solution. Beyond that, there is no need to look or expect. Be thankful that the way is being made so easy. You have much to thank me for, as you know full well in your heart.'

I saw Anthony Lycett smile, and yet he appeared reluctant to continue the conversation. But my Aunt Diane raised her face to his, and took his own face into her hands.

I saw his arms go around her, and their lips met. Their kiss was long and engrossing, and I did not wait to see them draw away.

CHAPTER THREE

During the next few days it seemed that Anthony Lycett called frequently at Rivermead House. Often he brought a gift for Lady Diane or myself; a small nosegay of flowers, a miniature book, a tiny thimble in a tapestry case. All his gifts were not of great value; yet it seemed that both Aunt Diane and I cherished them. We looked beyond the value to the goodwill they clearly expressed.

Lord Anthony spoke frequently about the war. 'The Duke of Wellington has already triumphed in Portugal, and has been well received in Cadiz and Lisbon. Praise has been heaped upon him, and now... Now the Battle of Victoria has been gained also, and great booty has been captured by the British forces.' It seemed that nothing could stem the triumphant British advance.

I looked forward to these visits by Lord Anthony. I had put from my mind the disturbing scene I had witnessed in the hall, late at night, after the reception at Lady

Effingham's. I had not been able to understand the words which had passed between Lord Anthony and my aunt; and even now, after thought, the meaning and import of their suggestions was obscure to me.

I told myself that manners were different in London, in court circles, from the customs prevalent at Pomfret Magna. There a kiss had significance; words uttered with intensity had meaning. But here, the scales seemed reversed, and values contradictory. I told myself that what I had witnessed and heard had been nothing more than *politeness*; even a game; a ploy in social intercourse. The scene could surely have no deeper significance.

Sir Toby had a position in the city of London, but what that was, I did not know. Yet he seemed often at home in the late afternoon, and then he would talk to me on general matters which interested him. He took me into his study, and showed me his books, his cases of butterflies, and his collection of foreign weapons. His hobby was the innocuous one of composing Latin verse; and he corresponded with a professor at Oxford, who received and commented upon his work.

We sat one day in the salon, taking a dish of tea together. Diane was not present. I did not know where she was. I noticed that she had these long, unexplained absences in her day.

'I see you have made a friend of Anthony Lycett,' Sir Toby said to me. 'Or he has made a friend of yourself. He is an agreeable person, Felicity, and no doubt you are envied to have his attentions. But perhaps one word of warning may be acceptable. I know you will take what I have to say in good part.'

He paused before continuing. 'To start with, Anthony Lycett, though a man about town and accepted at the royal court is impoverished. He has no private means at all.'

'Impoverished!' I cried. 'How can that be?' He had given me the impression of wealth in his keeping, or at least of adequate means. 'I know he is a serving soldier. And surely a soldier is adequately paid?'

'You are correct,' Sir Toby replied. 'Anthony Lycett is a captain attached to the Duke of Wellington's headquarters in London. But I do not know at all how seriously he takes this commission. I do not know what his functions may be in the Duke's service.

'His pay may be adequate for a young man without social commitments. But for one who frequents the Prince Regent's court ... The army levée will be inadequate indeed.'

I sat silent, considering this information. Sir Toby resumed, 'Anthony's only close relation, the Marquis of Glenivray has recently died. He was a wealthy man, but the estate is in the hands of lawyers. There is grave confusion over the will, and some say that Anthony will receive little of his uncle's estate.

'I mention these matters only to make you

aware of the position concerning your new friend. I would not wish you to make any mistakes from ignorance of the salient and obvious facts.'

Then suddenly Sir Toby's voice changed. A note of censure came into his speech. 'Anthony Lycett is also a womanizer and a rake. No charges have been brought against him by the ladies he has loved and discarded. They are too proud for that. Yet his reputation remains. Take care, Felicity. Be on your guard. Your new-found friend has a more devious nature than you might expect. I would not wish you to be deceived.'

Sir Toby then drew towards him the block of paper on which he composed his odes. I thanked him for his discourse, and withdrew.

I walked in the rear garden, towards the River Thames which flowed gently on the perimeter of the property. I realized that Sir Toby's information had affected me not at all.

I did not care that Anthony Lycett was of impoverished means. I was of impoverished means, myself. I knew all about scraping and saving and trying to put on a bold front, not for show, but to bolster the courage of the spirit within.

I admired him that he did not bow down before this adversity, but held his head high, and associated with his equals. I did not doubt but that he would receive promotion in his career as a soldier, and this would solve many of his problems. I discounted the further words which Sir Toby had added to his expressed disapproval of Sir Anthony.

'It is easy for a man of good birth to enter society and keep his place there. There are many usurers in London, who will support such a one, waiting for an inheritance, or a wealthy marriage.'

What Lord Anthony did was his own concern, I told myself. He was not one, I argued, to involve himself in mountainous debts, or a loveless union. I realized suddenly that he could do no wrong in my eyes. I was his secret champion. He found great favour in my sight. Indeed, my heart beat faster as I thought of him; and his handsome face and elegant form were re-created before me. My heart was drenched with sweetness as I thought of him, and I held the nosegay he had given me close to my face.

It was then a strange incident occurred, which I found difficult to understand. Mr Maurice Grosz came to dinner.

Mr Grosz was a lawyer, celebrated in financial and legal circles, I was informed. He was an acquaintance of Diane and Sir Toby; but Diane had met him at a dinner party and had invited him on impulse, so she said. He was a portly gentleman, with silver hair which he hid under a wig. He was one of the few men at this time who still wore the hair-piece, so fashionable in previous years. He looked rather like a learned judge about to pass sentence on some malefactor for stealing a sheep.

Naturally, the three of us set ourselves out to make Mr Grosz welcome, and to make the meal a pleasant one. When dinner was over, Mr Grosz took me by the arm, in a friendly but civil way, and steered me away from the table to an embrasure in the corner of the room.

He engaged me in conversation. He told anecdotes, and stories of his family. But at the same time, I noticed, he elicited from me much information about myself, my background, my interests, my beliefs and proclivities. Yet this was done so subtly, I did not realize how much I had revealed of my circumstances and myself, until a later time. I was puzzled by his interest in me, and my days at Pomfret Magna. How could my humble circumstances concern this doyen of legal circles, in London? Again, I was at a loss to understand the course of events.

But Diane seemed pleased by this conversation between Mr Grosz and myself. 'You entertained him royally, my dear,' she said. 'You are growing in social poise. This will stand you good stead in the future,' she added. She looked at me in a calculating way, which again, I could not understand.

And then occurred for me what was an event of great importance; something which seemed to shake my very being to its core. I fell in love.

I had not been in love before. But then, I had

met few men who might arouse my affections. But now, with the coming of Anthony Lycett into my life, it seemed that I had met the being who could stir my body, mind and personality to their very foundations. I felt indeed swept off my feet, and suspended in air.

The realization of my intense commitment occurred on the evening when the four of us had been invited to a levée at the Alderney Rooms. The Prince Regent was to be the host. 'And with luck,' Diane said, 'you might be presented to his Royal Highness. But not,' she added, 'if Mrs Fitzherbert sees you first.'

Her laughter rang out in the room. But it seemed to me that she was laughing at something undisclosed, and not admitted. And her gaiety did not reach her eyes.

* * *

I had wondered often about Diane's attitude towards Anthony Lycett, following the tableau I had seen in the hall; the kiss, the conversation, the obvious closeness. If she had an inclination towards him, which I had learned many married women at court felt towards other men, then she might not approve of his preference for me; and of his friendship which I felt was steadily and firmly growing.

But this was not the case. She did not appear to care that Anthony showed me favour.

Indeed, she seemed to go out of her way to foster our relationship; to make our friendship more firm, constant and abiding.

And this reinforced in me, of course, the conviction that relations between Diane and Anthony were trivial, of little consequence. Had she cared deeply for Anthony, I told myself, she would have blocked our path, not smoothed our way. Instead, our cordial relationship progressed beneath her kindly gaze. I sometimes thought that the adverse and puzzling incidents which I had recently encountered, had been a myth.

On this particular evening I dressed with care, hoping to make myself presentable for Anthony and Diane—for so, by her Christian name, my aunt wished me to address her. 'We will discard the "aunt" dear child,' she had informed me. 'I am not so aged, surely!'

Mr Percival arrived at around four o'clock to do the hair of Diane, and then of myself. He formed my hair into ringlets around my face with heated tongs and drew the frontispiece high, like a pomadour. Then this style did not please him, and he swept the whole of my tresses into a freefall of curls which reached my shoulders.

'I will not make you old before your time,' the coiffeur said. 'When you are a married woman will be time for a pompadour. But for now ... enjoy your youth and innocence,' he added with regret, and almost under his breath. 'Believe me, where you are going these are scarce and difficult to find.'

I went downstairs to the salon, to await the arrival of the other guests. I stood before a gilded Florentine mirror and regarded my reflection.

The dress of pale peach silk was indeed becoming; it was nipped in at the waist, with the skirt full and flowing. The *décolleté* was a trifle daring, I thought; I was not used to exposing my shoulders so generously. But Diane wore this style well, and she assured me that this was the custom in London. Ladies liked to display their attractions. It was considered dull and frowsy to cover up the upper arms.

So I had consented to the style. True, the bodice of the dress, trimmed with cream lace, was acceptable enough; though very revealing to the shape of the bosom. Yet the whole ensemble seemed artistic and beautifully sewn. And the colour seemed to complement the russet hues of my hair, and the pale sun-burnt colouring of my skin. I was thus engaged in cogitation, when I heard a sound behind me, and turned in surprise.

Anthony Lycett had entered the salon unannounced; yet not unwelcome. For pleasure flooded through me as I observed his face and form. I looked with approbation at his tall figure clad in the formal evening dress of the day: the long tight pale grey trousers, the cut-away coat of dark blue, the white silk shirt, pleated and ruffled, which seemed to set off the whole.

He smiled when he saw me; his pleasure seemed to match my own. I saw the gleam in his grey eyes, the lightening of his countenance when he smiled. He came towards me and took my hand.

'How entrancing you look this evening, Felicity,' he said. And though this was a formal compliment which I guessed had been uttered many times before without foundation, yet, at this moment, the words gave me joy; and I genuinely believed that I found favour in Anthony Lycett's eyes.

'Do you approve of my dress?' I asked. 'It is not too bold and extreme?'

'Not at all. The whole becomes you well. Diane has indeed had a willing pupil, and has instructed you to the benefit of you both.'

Then he seemed to regret mentioning Diane's name, for he said, 'I see you have no jewellery of consequence, Felicity, to add the final touch to your *toilette*. No doubt in Pomfret Magna personal decoration was not greatly approved. But here, in London, a touch of gold or precious stone is usual to add to the final effect. I have brought you this.'

And so saying, Anthony drew from an inner pocket a small case, on the lid of which was a gold crest. He opened the catch with a swift flick of his wrist, before placing the whole in my hands.

Within the case was a locket of gold, upon a filigree chain. In the centre of the locket a diamond shone, and around the diamond, the centre of the pendant was chased with an heraldic design.

I was speechless at the ornament before me. 'It is truly beautiful,' I stammered, quite at a loss for words. 'But I cannot believe that this is a gift, on so short acquaintance. Do you wish to loan this trinket to me, for this evening?' I looked up at his face. I held the case and the locket still undisturbed, in my hand.

'But no,' answered Anthony. 'This pendant is a gift indeed from myself, to you. It was once my mother's and has therefore great sentimental association for me. But I have thought the matter over, and I would like you to have her necklace. It will give me pleasure to see you wear it. And I know that with you, it will be in safe hands.'

Anthony then drew the locket from its case, and turned me around. He drew the golden chain around my neck, and fastened the clasp. He turned me again to look upwards into his face.

The whole incident had taken me by surprise. My reactions were uncertain. I sought in his own expression some indication as to what I should say. But Anthony Lycett gave me no time for words. He drew me into his arms, and placed his lips upon mine in a close

and demanding kiss.
He held me within the circle of his embrace, a prisoner close to his form. And I stood motionless, lost in the sensation of the moment, like one adrift upon a tide which was ebbing fast. It seemed in that moment that I had reached the point of no return.

CHAPTER FOUR

I was to learn later that there are many ways of falling in love. The long slow process, based upon mutual regard and affection. The sudden revelation of a close companion's new identity; the wild abandonment of the heart over a partner the rest of the world scorned. But I did not know of any of these occasions, at this moment. For as Anthony Lycett's lips found mine, as he held me in his intense embrace crushed to his heart, the whole of my life, and indeed my nature, was changed. It was in that moment that I fell wildly and deeply in love.

I felt my body respond to his closeness. I know that I trembled; a flush suffused my shoulders and face; an unfamiliar elation lifted both my spirits and my mind. When Anthony drew apart from me, and let me go, I in my turn took him into my arms. And I also implanted a kiss upon his face. He smiled as I did so, and when I drew apart he cried;

'Why Felicity! What ardour. What enthusiasm! You are a young lady of great depths. Beneath your proper exterior it is clear a warm and ardent nature exists, seeking only to be allowed the opportunity to reveal itself!'

He held me at arm's length; laughing at my by now slightly dishevelled appearance, and the flush which still dyed my face. It was at this moment that the door of the salon opened, and Lady Diane and Sir Toby entered the room.

Diane stopped, clearly greatly surprised by the tableau we presented. Then I saw her expression change. She was visibly displeased by our proximity, and obvious amity.

As she came closer, I saw her eyes rest upon the pendant upon my bosom. She turned from me so that I should not see the consternation in her eyes.

'Come now, we have no time for dalliance,' she cried, as if making light of the incident between Anthony and myself. 'Flirtations take up one's time, and time is pressing when the Prince Regent calls.

'Toby, please arrange Felicity's wrap. Anthony, kindly hand me my feathered shawl. The carriage is at the door. Let us away. This is a serious occasion, but then, all enjoyment is a serious affair.'

And so my aunt shepherded us out of the salon, along the hall to the front-door. As Anthony handed her into the coach I heard her say, very quietly to him;

'There is no need to overdo matters, my lord. It was not necessary to give her the late marchioness's pendant. You know I have always liked that bauble, and you promised... You know what you promised ... You promised that one day it would be mine...

'Please do not take unorthodox actions, or you will spoil everything. If things go wrong, you will have only yourself to blame.'

The scene at the Alderney Rooms was even more brilliant than the social scene I had witnessed before. Beneath the lights of these banqueting-rooms, the lavishly dressed throng moved with the studied restlessness of waters cast up by a fountain, or pebbles tossed upon a seashore. The dresses of the ladies were more colourful and extreme, to please his Royal Highness, who delighted in such displays and spectacles. The uniforms of the men and the liveries of the royal servants made a background to this dazzling and almost overwhelming display.

I saw at once that my entry with Lord Anthony Lycett caused comment; many eyebrows were raised, and remarks were made behind the screening of fans. Some were displeased at his escorting so new an arrival at the court of the Prince; others were curious, licentious, flippant, wondering.

I saw that Diane noticed these reactions, and she secretly smiled. I did not know what amused her, and indeed, her reactions to recent events puzzled me greatly. Also, her remarks to Anthony, made as he handed her into the carriage, were perplexing. I was at a loss to find any sense in her comments, at all.

Not that anything so trivial could spoil my pleasure in the evening, and the intense joy I found in being at Anthony's side! His courtliness, his easy grace and charm impressed me. He was obviously greatly at home in these circles, and was respected and liked by many in this sphere. I did not know that my admiration showed clearly upon my face. And that some looked with envy upon my unquestioning approval of Anthony Lycett, and the happiness he had already brought to my heart.

At the end of this room was a dais, upon which were arranged two large chairs, almost like thrones. These chairs were draped with brocade, and surrounded by an arrangement of ferns. In the foremost chair the Prince Regent was seated at ease, as he surveyed the scene before him. He turned his head frequently to speak to the man by his side.

I saw that the Prince Regent had been once a handsome man; slim, with fine features and of intelligent cast of mind. But the life he had pursued had taken its heavy toll; his body had thickened, his looks had been coarsened and lost. He appeared to be fighting a battle against boredom and lack of interest in his pursuits. Even this gathering, at which he was the host, seemed not to engage his attention or his mind.

I noticed with great interest the man beside the Prince. 'That is Beau Brummell,' my aunt whispered to me. 'Do not offend Beau Brummell, or you offend the Prince. The Beau is the Prince's confidant and mentor. If you please Beau, you will please the Prince Regent also.

'They were at Eton together, and have been firm friends ever since. But the Beau is not merely a fop as many assume. He is a classical scholar, and a man of dignity and sensibility. Do not underestimate Beau Brummell, ever. He is more than a match for all the conspirators, here.'

I looked then with interest at the Prince's companion. He was tall and slender; his skin rather pale, his eyes brown, as was his hair. He wore an unusual evening jacket of dark blue, with tight breeches to match. Upon his feet and legs were elegant boots of white leather. The whole had a touch of rather *outré* elegance; yet the costume was not incongruous; it was not overdone. He inclined his head as he made some telling remark to his patron, the Prince.

And now we saw that both Beau Brummell and the Prince Regent were looking in our direction. It was as if our own scrutiny had drawn their eyes. The Prince, after consulting Beau, turned his head to a footman, and gave a directive. Within a few moments the flunkey was at our side.

'His Royal Highness presents his compliments to Sir Toby and Lady Bullough, and asks to receive their house guest, Miss Felicity Lowe.'

'If you will come this way, sir, with the ladies, I will conduct you into His Highness's presence,' the footman said. He bowed his bewigged and powdered head, and began to lead the way.

It was as if the whole assembly knew of the summons to my Aunt Diane, to bring me to the Prince Regent's notice. A path was cleared for us, as escorted by my aunt and Sir Toby, we began to make our way towards the dais.

I tried to still the fluttering which assailed me, telling myself that the Prince was a man like any other, that I must not be dismayed, that I must conduct myself formally, so as to be equal to the occasion. And then I was curtseying before the dais, and his Royal Highness put out his hand, and raised me to my feet.

I saw that the Prince was clad in brown, with big brass buttons on his jacket, with heavy rings upon his pudgy fingers, and huge buckles upon his shoes. 'So this is Lady Bullough's niece from the country,' he began. He had a pleasant tenor voice, and he smiled at me in an agreeable way. 'One could have expected a bumpkin, eh, Beau, but this young lady is a beauty, is she not? You have taken us all by surprise. And your charms are not less agreeable by being unusual and intriguing.

'That colour, eh Beau? That satin skin, like a peace itself surrounded by dark leaves! The hair, Beau! Don't you see it? As one who came second in the Newdigate Prize at Oxford, you are slow this evening to appreciate poetry when you hear it. Or do you consider you could do better yourself? Come let me hear it. Praise this young lady before us in verse.'

Beau Brummell was not put out by this discourse; nor did he rise to the Prince's sallies. His eyes upon me were steady and penetrating; I thought he had great understanding of the human mind. He whispered something I was sure was not concerned with myself, and made the Prince laugh. After a few moments of general conversation in which Lady Diane and Sir Toby were included, the Prince bowed, which was our signal that we must retire.

Anthony Lycett now joined us, as we stood for a few moments to recover from our audience with the Prince. It was then I heard, quite distinctly, a further conversation between the Prince and Beau Brummell.

'So this is the pretty chicken who will rescue Lycett,' the Prince said ruminatively. 'Yet she presents no hardship, surely. Many men would be pleased to meet his fate without any strings attached.'

'I do not approve,' said Beau Brummell austerely. 'The Marquis was a boor and a prig to make this charade necessary. And there is always risk of hurt in these affairs,' the celebrated dandy continued. 'Not merely to the young lady in question, but who knows, Lycett himself may come off worse.'

'Since when have you suffered by proxy, Beau?' the Prince replied. 'This dainty piece is set to cheat me, Beau, but so guileless and fresh is she, I cannot hold it against her.

'And speaking of wine, Beau, or were we? Call the footman. I have recently taken delivery of a cellar in St James's of...'

The Prince's voice tailed away. But Beau Brummell's reply was clearly heard:

'I think Lycett may get more than he bargains for with her, if he pursues his course. This dove may peck him and draw blood when he least expects it. I would not like to be in his shoes when he is called to account.'

The import of these words was lost upon me; I did not turn my head to look again at the Prince and Beau Brummell, for I felt this would be out of place and inquisitive. We all adjourned to the supper-room. And later I was presented to Mrs Fitzherbert, whose beauty, grace and style greatly impressed me. But she appeared abstracted, and though civil was not forthcoming. But when I regarded the scene in the main chamber of the Alderney Rooms, I understood her perturbation and the preoccupation of her mind.

For though Lady Effingham was present at this reception also, the Prince Regent did not show favour to either Lady Effingham, or to Mrs Fitzherbert herself. He appeared to spend the entire evening talking to Beau Brummell; and that their amity was close, was clear for all to see.

Later I saw the Prince engage in conversation a beautiful young lady stylishly dressed and very appealing. I was told that this was the Duchess of Rutland. But the Duchess too, the Prince dismissed with his courtly bow. He drank alone with Beau, regarding with his jaundiced eye the revels of the guests and the brilliant social scene. He appeared to me to have considerable matters, undisclosed, upon his mind, and engaging his private attention.

Lady Diane was skilled in these social affairs, and soon after my presentation to the Prince she suggested that we should depart. She also had discerned the Prince's ennui, and guessed that soon he would leave the Rooms and the evening would diminish. We made our way back to Rivermead House and there Anthony bade us goodnight, without waiting for the customary nightcap, or any further conversation.

He did not of course, bid me farewell in any too friendly or intimate way. And I was now well enough versed in the customs of this circle to accept his reserve. Yet his hand held mine for longer than the customary time; and his eyes searched and lingered upon my face. Our eyes met, and much that was secret was expressed in our private and hidden glance.

Alone in my bedroom, when I had removed my tight stays and the stiff brocade of the dress which had held my figure in a vice, I allowed myself the luxury of giving rein to my feelings. I remembered the moments between Anthony and myself, when he had placed the treasured locket around my neck; and when he had drawn me close to him, and had implanted his kiss upon my lips.

I remembered the wild sensation his embrace had occasioned within me. It was like the eruption of a volcano, my responses; a volcano one had not suspected, or that threatened with its fire beneath the rectitude of normal life.

I traced, as I got into bed, the emotions which had assailed me, since I had arrived upon the London scene. The shyness, trepidation, hesitations; my gratitude towards Lady Diane and Sir Toby; my realization of the pitfalls and treacheries of court society; my deepening friendship with Anthony which had so taken me by surprise.

And now his gift of a pendant, and his searching and demanding kiss. And my self-shattering and overwhelming response. The whole relationship seemed to have the unreality of a dream, I thought; as sleep itself, in my bed, threatened to overtake me. It was hard to accept as reality the circumstances of my relationship with Anthony Lycett.

The shortness of our acquaintanceship, I thought. The fact that he was a man of social eminence, of high degree in the circles attached to the royal court. How had he come to look with favour upon myself, an unschooled girl straight from the country, unused to the nuances and rules of the life into which he had been born? The whole matter seemed highly unlikely; and yet it had occurred. Again I could not understand the situation. I could only accept the events; and thank heaven for the bliss which had been occasioned within me by Anthony's persistence in seeking my friendship, and by the latest token of his regard.

I fell asleep at last, not remembering the conversation between the Prince and Beau Brummell which concerned myself. I was later to remember the Beau's shadowed eyes as he had regarded me. I was later to give credence to the meaning of his low-toned words.

CHAPTER FIVE

The next morning there was a letter from my Aunt Rebecca. I was glad to receive it, for in spite of my preoccupations in London, I had missed her greatly, and in private moments memories of our lives together in Pomfret Magna returned with unexpected force.

Yes, I had been homesick. I had longed for our settled days and the uncomplicated nature of our existence. Here, in circles attached to the court, there were pitfalls, deceit, I felt; treachery and dissimulation. But in Pomfret Magna people lived their lives more honestly; they were accepted at face value; we were open books to each other. Kindliness reigned; succour in adversity, and understanding of the daily dilemmas of country life.

I tore the epistle open eagerly, picturing my aunt's face and form in my mind; and the parlour in which she would have written the letter. But the contents astounded me.

' ... a Mr Grosz has been here, enquiring about you, Felicity. He wished to know all the details of your life, your friends, and particularly men friends, and all the pursuits in which your days had been spent.

'I told him that your only man friend had been Mr Hubbard, your mentor, who had wished to become engaged to you, in the distant future, when you were of an age for this. Had any closeness taken place? Mr Grosz asked me. And of course I answered, you were unsullied in mind and body in every way.

'Then I wondered why I was answering these questions. But truth to tell, I found Mr Grosz rather intimidating, and I could not think of a way of evading his questions without offending someone of clearly eminent position.

'I was told he is a legal gentleman of some

prominence in London. He came in a beautiful carriage, with a legal clerk who attended him, and searched the parish registers on his behalf. He had two footmen on the carriage, in full livery. I did not learn his official position. He came for information, not to give it. And when he was satisfied with my responses to his enquiries, he thanked me gravely, and went away.

'He left behind a case of dry sack wine, for my pains, he said. But I have not opened this, Felicity, for I do not know the truth of the matter upon which this lawyer is engaged.

'If you can enlighten me, please do so. For I am greatly in the dark, and the questioning left me perturbed in mind, and uneasy for you in my heart.'

The letter continued with family and village matters. I laid the pages down.

I determined that I must try and seek some enlightenment on these puzzling matters which surrounded me. And I determined to seek my Aunt Diane without delay.

But she was not to be found. Bloomingfield told me that she was absent upon an unexplained occasion. As this happened frequently, no-one made any comment, or had any explanations of her movements or her errands.

To while away the time until Diane's return, I roamed through the big house. And again, a circumstance which had struck me earlier, returned to my consciousness and my attention.

Away from the main rooms of the house, Rivermead House was, beneath its outward luxury and show, run-down and dilapidated. The gilt was peeling from the mirrors and ornaments; the decorations were scuffed, the upholstery of the *chaise-longues* and sofas threadbare and faded.

It is true, at first the whole house had struck me with its grandeur and luxury. And indeed, that was the impression it still presented to the casual eye. But to one who scrutinized more closely, it was apparent that beneath the façade, there was dilapidation and neglect. It seemed that money at Rivermead House was running low.

I remembered, in my perambulation around the house, an incident I had witnessed only recently between Sir Toby and Bloomingfield. The tall, formidable upper servant had said, 'I must ask you for my wages, again. I cannot go longer without my stipend for my work. I have dependants. A sick mother, a lame sister. I request you again to reimburse me for my arrears, and the latest payment which is now due.'

I did not know what Sir Toby had said; he had mumbled something in reply, and had ambled off. He had gone into the study to engage himself with his Latin verse, no doubt; but a troubled impression was left upon

my mind.
Yet there was so much that could be done to ease the situation, I thought, as I progressed throughout the house. Brocade curtains could be mended; cushions fashioned to hide the fraying tapestries; even the carpets could be stitched with stout thread to draw together the unserviceable parts. But when my Aunt Diane arrived from her unspecified engagement, she seemed not in any mood to hear my suggestions or ideas.
She was elegantly dressed; no doubt she had been paying a call upon some woman friend at court. She drew aside her cloak to reveal her dress of green velvet, trimmed with lace. I saw a neck ornament shine upon her bosom and around her neck.
'Please do not plague me with such novelties, Felicity,' she cried, when she had heard me out. 'No lady ever works with her hands. Please remember that. As for renovating the house... Wait a while. I assure you that shortly, in time, this will be done.'
She seemed about to say more, indeed I heard her begin '... where you are going manual work will not be necessary...' then she curbed her utterances, as if she overstepped the barriers she had placed upon herself. She turned from me with impatience and made her way up the stairs.
It was not until she had gone that I realized I had not asked her about Mr Grosz. When she

came downstairs again, in a less elaborate dress of blue, for it was still only mid-afternoon, I put my questions to her. She could see I was perturbed, and sought some explanation of these circumstances puzzling both to my Aunt Rebecca and myself.

But Diane dismissed my anxieties. 'I assure you I have no knowledge of Mr Grosz' movements—if it were he.

'I doubt very much that Mr Grosz would travel to the west country on an errand so vague and unexplained. No doubt this gentleman was an agent from the landlord who owns property in the village. Or does your aunt have debts? Was he a collector or dun, who sought settlement of some account?

'Please do not vex me with these matters, Felicity. I assure you I have other, more urgent concerns upon my mind.'

I felt rebuffed, and turned to go. But something in my aunt's expression stayed me. And I felt sure that she was lying. She knew of the situation well, but was not going to reveal any truth to me.

She swept away with a swirl of her flowing skirts. I heard her talking to Bloomingfield in the distance. Her voice was acrimonious, and so was Bloomingfield's reply. I thought that there would be trouble in this household from Bloomingfield before long.

Just at this moment the study-door opened, and Sir Toby entered the hall, accompanied by another man.

I looked at the stranger with interest; for he was an unusual sight, though it was difficult to trace what his peculiarities were. He was fashionably dressed and moved gracefully. He was middle-aged, with an eye for the ladies. He bowed when he saw me, but Sir Toby did not present us to one another. I watched Sir Toby escort the stranger to the door.

'A friend with whom I play chess,' said Sir Toby easily, though I noticed his face was flushed, and he appeared ill at ease.

'We discuss the war too. He is a member of my club. He is well informed.'

Sir Toby took my arm. 'This war in Portugal,' he said. 'This tricky Lisbon peninsula. Yet it is all part of the great design. The conquest of Europe, and then the conquest of these islands! The French are behind everything. Never trust a Frenchman, my dear. The Duke of Wellington knows better than to take them at their word.

'And now, my work at the Ministry is done for the day,' he added. 'A little relaxation with my Latin Verses follows. And then the despatch of my portfolio for Oxford!'

Sir Toby left me rather abruptly, I thought, and entered the study and closed the door.

It was then I realized that my Aunt Diane awaited me. I saw that she had changed her dress yet again, as if for some important event or occasion. The expression on her face was pleasant and anticipatory too.

It was as if she had accepted some course, and was now pursuing the action with a kind of perverted enjoyment or relish. I could not understand her attitude, or the rapid changes of her moods. She placed her hand upon my arm, and drew me into the salon. She turned to face me, smiling into my eyes.

'Brace yourself for some news, dear Felicity,' she said. 'News of a startling kind, which must bring you great happiness.' She paused. 'Lord Anthony Lycett has asked my permission, as your immediate guardian, to approach you with a request for an engagement. Yes Felicity, Lord Anthony Lycett wishes to marry you. He wishes to approach you to ask you to become his wife.'

* * *

To say that I was astounded would be an under description. Surprise of such intensity flooded through me, it was like an attack of ague, or an onset of some dementia. I could not speak. I was bereft of words. I could only stare at my aunt's smiling and amiable face.

'Lord Anthony asked me to attend him at Beaufroy House, this afternoon. Beaufroy House is the home of his uncle, the Marquis, now deceased, where Anthony is lodging at the present time.

'And there he told me of his affection for

you, and of his wish that you should marry, and share your lives together. Come, Felicity. Say something. This intelligence has not made you dumb, surely! Tell me what is in your mind?'

'But we have known each other for so short a time!' I cried. 'How can Lord Anthony be sure of his feelings for me?

'And he is so above me,' I cried. 'He is a nobleman, whereas I am connected to no eminent family. Saving yourself, Diane, and Sir Toby. And there is a difference in our ages. And he has the whole of London society to choose from! How can he possibly prefer such a person as myself!

'And I have no dowry. No settlements. I cannot understand the circumstances.' My words ran out, but my perturbation and puzzlement remained clear I knew upon my face and in my eyes.

'Tell me, Felicity,' my aunt said, 'what are your feelings for Anthony? Tell me frankly please, I wish to know.'

'I love him,' I said. 'I love him truly. He is the first man in my life to bring me pleasure and happiness. I should be overjoyed to be his wife.'

'Just as I thought,' my Aunt Diane said. 'But say no more at this time, dear child. For Anthony is coming to the early dinner this evening, and seeks to see you alone after the meal.'

My aunt drew me close and kissed me. 'I wish you happiness, truly, my dear,' she said. 'I have your interests at heart. You will realize all this, in time.

'But now, go to prepare yourself for your meeting with Anthony. I will send Bloomingfield to help you. It is not too early. Borrow my tongs to wind up your hair, and rub yourself all over, before you begin your *toilette*, with eau de Cologne.'

My aunt's benevolence astounded me. Her graciousness towards me concerning my prospective engagement to Anthony removed all doubts from my mind. I sped away to do her bidding.

There were no hesitations within me; no doubts; no pausing for second thoughts. Gladness of such intensity flooded through me, it seemed that all that had gone before had been a myth, a dream, a chimera. This was the reality, I thought, as Bloomingfield arrived with the hot towel and the perfume. She spoke little as she wound the tongs around my long and free-flowing hair.

CHAPTER SIX

The evening meal with Anthony present was inevitably a muted affair. But Sir Toby uncorked some rare wine; and Bloomingfield had polished the silver and plate. Afterwards, Diane and Sir Toby quitted the salon, and gave Anthony and myself the opportunity to be together.

'Your aunt will have told you, without doubt,' he said, 'of my wish for our betrothal. Do you agree, Felicity? Will you marry me? Will you accept me as your husband, and be my wife?'

'But of course,' I answered, and went at once to his side. I thought he would take me into his arms and kiss me, but he did not do that. He stood quite still and regarded me gravely. Then he raised his hand, and touched my hair. He leaned forward, and placed a chaste kiss upon my brow.

I myself took his hand in mine. 'I am certain of our happiness,' I said. 'I am skilled in all the housewifely arts, and can do everything that is now required of a woman.

'Also, I am aware you are a serving soldier, under the command of the Duke of Wellington. Please let me tell you what I have in mind.

'Sir Toby says that shortly the reserves will be going to serve on relief duties overseas in Madrid. If this is so, I could go with you. I could become an army wife. For as you know, many women travel abroad with their men these days. I could accompany you and aid you in everything you have to do.'

'Felicity, allow me to speak,' Anthony

answered. 'You are assuming I shall have only my army pay. But perhaps, by some circumstance, my station might improve. I cannot say more now. But it is possible ... Trust me please. I cannot elaborate further, or ask you more than this, at this time.'

I was puzzled by the ambiguity of this statement; but the pleasure of the circumstances continued to fill my mind. Yet I had made the offer of my wifely services to the man I loved. I felt that I too could do no more than this. We had both committed ourselves to one another, as far as we could, at the present time.

I now certainly expected Anthony to embrace me; to produce a ring for my finger, or some piece of jewellery to seal our troth. But he appeared abstracted. He did not approach me; and when Diane entered the room, he made his excuses, and went away.

My doubts at Anthony's strange behaviour were overcome by joy in my engagement to him. I wrote to my Aunt Rebecca, to tell her of my betrothal, and alert her to the possibility of my marriage in due course. But my Aunt Diane's next move caused me considerable surprise.

She came to me within two or three days, and said, 'Anthony wishes for an immediate ceremony, Felicity. He desires that you and he should be married within the next few days.'

'But how could this be arranged?' I asked.

'What of the preliminaries? My trousseau! The presence of my Aunt Rebecca! Why does he wish this haste? Surely he can grant me a little time?'

'I understand the haste is due to some matter concerning Anthony's service with the Duke of Wellington. You know there is secrecy in military matters. But possibly Anthony is due to take up a command abroad,' she said vaguely.

'He has not told me the exact reason,' she added glibly. 'But he has asked me to prepare you for his request for an early ceremony to make you man and wife.'

Of course I agreed. When Anthony called to see me later that day, I acceded at once to his request. And a date was fixed for our nuptials for the following week.

I could not understand the haste. Even with unspecified military service pressing upon my future bridegroom, an engagement of at least a few months was customary at this time. My Aunt Diane seemed to set at naught my wishes for at least a new dress to be married in. 'It is not necessary, my dear,' she said.

'The ceremony is to be a quiet one, in the private chapel at Beaufroy House. Did you know there is a family chapel attached to the late Marquis's residence? But of course you did not know this. You have never seen Beaufroy House. But you will in due time. And you will approve what you will see.'

I thought her hesitation about new clothes for my wedding stemmed from reluctance to assume a debt she might have to be responsible for. But I had a little savings, and I insisted upon a new dress, and I told my aunt that I would pay.

So the dressmaker arrived with her patterns and her dolls. 'It must be of white satin trimmed with cream lace,' my aunt said. 'This colour will emphasize your...' I thought she was going to say virginity, but instead she hastily added '... your innocence and freshness.' And within a few days the dress arrived; and this matter was settled in my troubled and perplexed mind.

I could not understand why Anthony did not come to see me, and share in my joy. I had always understood that the period of engagement was a happy time for both parties. But here I was alone, and my fiancé was notably absent from my side.

I also felt there was much to discuss. Where would we live? Was military departure imminent? Was I to be forced back upon Aunt Rebecca or Aunt Diane, through lack of funds? Was our future in England or overseas? I felt that I was being kept in the dark upon vital matters. Matters which deeply concerned the wife, who must be responsible for the home, and the care of her husband's personal and intimate life.

Yet nothing was vouchsafed for me.

Everyone I met seemed part of this aura of silence. I began to approach my wedding day with apprehension and dismay.

Yet upon the day itself, nothing could dim my happiness at the thought of being united with Anthony in matrimony, and of sharing our life together. It seemed that naught in life could dim my prospects or rob me of the raptures to come.

* * *

Bloomingfield helped me to dress in her usual taciturn way. My white dress, with its long and flowing veil—a touch which was just coming into fashion with the ladies of the court—fell about my shoulders and down my back. I wore the locket which Anthony had given me. I had no other ornament save my mother's bracelet. I awaited the golden band upon my finger which would give me new status, and my entry into a new life.

The carriage had been especially spruced up, and its rather jaded paint cleaned and the dingy upholstery freshened. I travelled with both my Aunt Diane and Sir Toby. The servants wished me well. Bloomingfield alone stood at the rear with a sour and cynical expression upon her face.

We travelled through the streets of Richmond, and entered the purlieus of the city of London. We reached finally an old district called New Gate. And so we drew up in the front of Beaufroy House.

I was amazed by the size and style of this mansion. It was clearly of great antiquity, blackened by the smoke of London's fires and torches; with eyes blind behind shutters and with a vast front door at the top of a ring of steps.

So this is where the old Marquis, now dead, had lived, I thought. And this is where Anthony lodged in a room at the present time. But I had no time for further cogitations, for the steps of the coach had been lowered, and Sir Toby was helping me to alight.

Inside the hall of this vast place, it was cold and rather dark. I saw a vast flight of marble steps leading to a gallery; many rooms opening off a lofty landing. Stone statues, oil paintings, oriental vases and candelabra were on view. And then Anthony was coming towards me, and everything else was forgotten as I saw the man I loved approach me upon the most momentous occasion of our lives.

He wore the uniform of a serving officer in the Duke of Wellington's own regiment. His coat was red, and heavily frogged; his breeches white, and his boots of shining black leather. He wore his sword, for this was a ceremonial occasion. He put out his hand and took my hand into his own. He raised my hand to his lips; and I felt the warmth and pressure of his lips upon my palm.

I saw that his fair hair was well brushed, and his grey eyes were alight with some hidden emotion. How dearly he must love me, I thought. He is already anxious to make me his wife. He is looking forward eagerly to the moment when he will make me his own.

Pleasure ran through my body also; and I had to restrain myself to stand still. Then Anthony gave me his arm, and followed by my Aunt Diane and Sir Toby, we progressed through the great hall of Beaufroy House, and approached the private chapel.

It was beautiful in design, with stained-glass windows letting in mauve, rose and golden lights. A small organ played. A ring of guests awaited us with grave and patient faces.

I saw a small group of servants, ancient in mien, and bowed with their years. One or two of Anthony's officer friends were there; an acquaintance of Lady Diane's, a friend of Sir Toby's. I, of course, had no friends present, nor relation. Aunt Diane had refused to allow Aunt Rebecca to be sent for. I approached the priest down the central aisle of this church on the arm of Anthony alone.

Yet I could not help but see a small group of men, clad in sombre garments, who were clearly professional men of some kind. Lawyers or men of affairs in banking or commerce. I was later to learn that these were the members of the late Marquis's trust; but I did not know this now.

And so the ceremony began. Short, but wonderfully moving. The ring was placed upon my finger. Anthony accorded me the customary formal kiss. And so I wed the man I loved; with my future still obscure.

The elderly major-domo called Benjamin, and Mrs Colgate, the housekeeper, had prepared wine and a cold collation in the drawing-room of the huge house. A small fire burned in the marble grate, which did not disturb the chill.

It was now being born upon me that Anthony and I must spend our wedding night within the confines of this mansion. And then we must discuss the future, I thought. I must know my responsibilities, and where these must take place.

Within a short space of time, the party broke up. 'If we may ask you to attend us in the study,' one of the dark-robed men, said to Anthony. 'We can complete the formal contracts. Only your signature is required, and the signatures of the trustees, also. All else is done, and has been for sometime.'

This gentleman bowed to Anthony, and then turned and bowed deeply to myself. With a shock I realized that this was Mr Grosz.

* * *

Anthony then left the small assembly, and accompanied Mr Grosz and other members of the trust to the study. There was some delay, and during this time, the small wedding party melted gradually away.

The last to leave were my Aunt Diane and Sir Toby. The latter seemed distressed to take his leave of me. 'I have enjoyed your presence in my household, Felicity,' he said. 'You have brought brightness and gaiety to our home. And your zest for life and all its experience has been a tonic to one who had become jaded. God be with you and aid you in your new life.'

My Aunt Diane was brightness itself; she appeared almost feverish in her hectic attitude. She patted my shoulders and pulled at my dress. Something very deep was in her mind, I thought, to make this exaggerated display of affection and concern, necessary.

And then everyone had gone. Even the members of the trust had taken their leave of me. They had bowed deeply, saying but few words. They carried with them sheaves of papers and documents. I saw the seals at the end of the red tapes, hanging free, as they quitted the house. And then Anthony and I were alone.

Although this was not strictly the time or the place, I was later to realize, yet I could not stop myself from asking some of the urgent questions in my mind.

'It is no doubt very kind of the members of your late uncle's trust to allow us to spend a few days here together, after our marriage,' I said. 'But the question of our future domicile remains unsolved. Please tell me, Anthony, where we are to live? What are our future means to be? I long to know, so that I may prepare myself for what is to come.'

Anthony came close to me, and smiled. I smelled the faint fumes of wine upon his breath; but his eyes also were bright, and shining with the certainty of inner knowledge.

'Do not concern your beautiful head with any conjectures about our future,' he said. 'For I am now the Marquis of Glenivray, and I have become my uncle's heir.

'I have inherited Beaufroy House, his estates in the country, and all his wealth. The papers have just been signed. The whole, the total will shortly be mine! There is no concern necessary for the future in any way at all.'

So saying, Anthony kissed my cheek, but in a pleasant, rather informal way; as one will kiss an elderly relation upon departing. He then turned and left me, and I stood still, looking after his retreating form.

* * *

Mrs Colgate came, and conducted me upstairs. We passed up the enormous marble staircase, to the distant gallery beyond. The room to which she conducted me was also large; furnished in a rather Tudor style, yet with a big double-bed in the centre, against one wall. The shades were drawn, though it was still afternoon. A small fire burned in the wide, white grate.

I found that my clothes and belongings were unpacked, and were hanging in the wardrobe. How pitiful and inadequate they looked in the immensity of the interior! I wondered whether to change my dress or not. I had no one to consult. I was at a loss as to what to do. Then I decided to continue to wear my wedding gown. This was a festive occasion after all, I told myself. There must be a pleasurable evening ahead for my new bridegroom and myself. I brushed my hair and dusted a little orris root upon my face. I then went down the marble stairs and entered the drawing-room.

It was empty. The dining-room also. I rang the bell for the servants, but no-one came. I finally sat beside the dying embers of the fire; awaiting events; awaiting Anthony; awaiting some signal as to what I was to do. But none came. No-one entered. I was left alone.

I thought at last that surely a meal must be served; I had eaten but little at the wedding reception, and knew Anthony also had had almost nothing to eat. But no food was served; no meal announced. Again the servants did not attend. At last, late in the evening, I went up the staircase to bed, alone.

I lay at last in the big double bed, in my new night shift of fine silk, which I had ordered from the dressmaker. I could not sleep, but lay awake, listening for a footstep outside the door; the sound of someone in the hall below; a voice, a cry, a presence in this upper floor of the house. But there was nothing.

I fell asleep at last, worn out with waiting and expecting Anthony to come. I awoke at dawn, but I was still alone.

Tears flooded my eyes that my wedding night had not taken place. I had longed ardently to give myself to my new husband; and receive his commitment in return. But outside, in the dawn, I could see the distant roofs of other houses in New Gate. I was alone. The house was silent. My marriage had not been consummated.

I fell back upon my pillows, and again tears ran from my eyes, wetting further my sodden pillow. I was now a marchioness, I told myself. But I was also a woman rejected, and alone. Nothing could take away my hurt and distress, I told myself. There was no greater shame or denial that a woman could experience. The morning came; yet I seemed to lack the strength to arise, and face the day.

CHAPTER SEVEN

One thinks that one cannot go on. One tells oneself it is not possible to resume life, or to go through the motions of existence. And yet, within a short time I got up from my bed, made my *toilette*, and went downstairs.

The house was empty, except for old Benjamin and Mrs Colgate, who were going about their duties in a half-hearted way. I wondered how they had managed to keep the giant premises so clean, if they had only themselves to rely on. Mrs Colgate brought me a dish of chocolate and some fresh bread and preserve; and after this I began the tour of inspection of Beaufroy House.

I passed from room to room, scarcely noting what I saw. Why had Anthony married me, then? I asked myself, as I examined the furniture and ornaments. I remembered the sly looks; the nods and winks. 'Here is a pretty capon ready for the plucking.' 'Rather a dove taken from its cote and ready to be ringed on both feet.' What had these comments meant, what had been the inference behind the words? 'He will gain so much and the penalty is not too severe, surely.'

I had longed ardently to experience the pleasures of married life. I had yearned to give myself in the surrender of love; and receive Anthony's personal pledging of himself in return. This should surely have been the signal experience of my life. But it had not taken place; and there was no explanation as to why this expected experience had been denied me. Small wonder I roamed as a ghost through the vast premises, and the luxury around me brought me neither pleasure nor consolation.

Mrs Colgate saw my preoccupation and withdrawal. She offered to make me a light luncheon, but this I declined. 'There will be the usual dinner in the dining-room at six o'clock,' the old retainer told me. 'The late marquis liked his guests to dress for this meal, and I believe the new marquis expects the same.'

The words were kindly spoken, and I went upstairs to change my dress and prepare for Anthony's arrival. Just before six o'clock, he arrived in a great hurry, and bearing a sheaf of spring flowers, which he presented to me.

'How can I apologize for my absence?' he cried. 'Yesterday after the ceremony, I had to go to Lincoln's Inn Fields to visit the chambers of Mr Grosz. At his instigation, there was further business to transact with the trustees. Documents to sign. Forms to be attested, oaths to be witnessed. The time flew by. We took a light meal in the chambers, and then...

'Then I called at the barracks of my regiment, on the way back to Beaufroy House. And there, my brother officers were waiting for me. They confiscated my jacket and breeches, and would not allow me to leave the barracks. It was their idea of a jape. They meant well, but their hilarity was misplaced.

'Their horseplay angered me, yet without my clothing I could not say them nay. I apologize most deeply, dearest Felicity. Say I am forgiven. Believe me, I would not hurt or offend you for a kingdom. Say I am pardoned, and I have your approval and regard, as before.'

Beneath the torrent of these words and explanations, my hurt and disappointment melted away. Anthony drew me into his arms, and kissed me; and I responded with some of my old eagerness to his kiss and embrace.

We entered the dining-room and began our meal. It was well cooked and beautifully served; but the viands were meagre and the menu parsimonious.

Afterwards, when we went into the drawing-room, I began to speak to Anthony.

'If Beaufroy House is to be our permanent home, I must ask you if some improvements and additions can be made to the establishment.

'We need renovations to the furniture and premises. Some redecoration. And Mrs Colgate and Benjamin need more staff. Have we the means for this? Is money available to make the premises more congenial?' I wondered then, if I had done the right thing in making this request.

Anthony sprang to his feet, and came to my side. 'But of course, Felicity. Anything you ask. You shall have a free rein to make what additions you wish. Do not hesitate. Money is no problem. Indeed...'

He threw up his hands. 'There is money in abundance for all that we shall need or require.

I told you already that I have inherited my uncle's estates. There is money from abroad, money from property in this country, money in banks and security houses—all soon to come into my hands. Do not hesitate, my darling. Whatever you wish now, shall be yours.'

I felt some happiness at these words, for in a strange way, while I had toured the great house, I had seen its potential as a family home; and its undoubted grace and beauty had interested and intrigued me.

Yet more than this, I longed that this night we should be united. I longed, I dared to hope, that later this evening we should become man and wife. The prospect caused both expectancy and hope within my heart.

Yet at nine o'clock, Anthony said, 'I regret I must leave you for a while. I have a long-standing engagement at a gentleman's dinner at Buck's Club. It concerns the regiment, and I cannot avoid it.

'I shall not be late, I trust, yet do not wait up for me, my dear. I will sleep in the dressing-room, so that I shall not wake you.

'If not tonight, I will see you tomorrow, dear Felicity. Sleep well, and pleasant dreams.'

And so the husband I loved so ardently, left me. And I knew, whatever his venue, he would not return to me that night.

Alone in my empty room, as I prepared for bed, I considered the courses of action open to me. I could leave Beaufroy House as quietly as

I had entered it, and make my way back to Pomfret Magna, and my Aunt Rebecca. Yet what excuse could I make for this journey? How to justify my presence in my old home?

I was a woman scorned by her husband; and unfulfilled, albeit pleasantly disregarded. All advice would be for me to return to Beaufroy House. Not all goes easily early in a marriage, I would be told. Patience. Return. Take up your position. Wait.

I could not bear the humiliation of such a situation. I did not want anyone to know of my disgrace.

For yes, so it seemed to me; a disgrace had descended upon me for which I was not prepared. As I put out the lamp and got into bed, I pondered yet another possibility. Yet I could not bear that my Aunt Diane and Sir Toby should know of this predicament. I could not bear that from me, the royal court of the Prince Regent should be given ammunition for their innuendos and sly tales.

As I lay in the darkness, I decided what I must do. I am the Marchioness of Glenivray, I told myself. Anthony Lycett of his own volition asked me to marry him, and this I have done. The title and position as his wife are legally mine. Mine is the duty now to uphold this name, and to bring what lustre I can, to this position for us both.

Proceed in life as if this intimate situation does not exist. Keep the dire secret hidden.

There are skeletons in all cupboards; no-one makes the disabilities of their life known.

And so I fell asleep with this conviction and determination strong within me. Yet when I awoke next morning to face the new day, the way ahead seemed hard, and life appeared without comfort and hope.

* * *

Within a few days Anthony told me that we had been invited by my Aunt Diane and Sir Toby to Rivermead House, for the evening dinner. He appeared pleased by this invitation, and I dressed with care, wishing to make a good impression upon our hosts, and please Anthony by my *toilette*. This was my first visit to my relations as a married woman, and I wished to behave with dignity, and comport myself well.

When we arrived at Rivermead House, I was astounded by what I saw. Within a few days, the exterior of the house had been redecorated; and inside the house, a great deal of renovation had taken place.

I saw new furnishings; bronze figures and ornaments; the flash of gold from ormolu clocks and mirrors; the smell of enamel and fresh greenery.

Aunt Diane greeted me civilly, and seemed pleased to see me again. 'It is quiet without you, Felicity,' Sir Toby said. 'I miss you, my dear. But my loss is no doubt Anthony's gain.'

I could not help but mention the lavish improvements to the house. Diane laughed rather uneasily, I thought. 'Sir Toby has had a windfall,' she told me. 'An old aunt in Edinburgh has died, and has left him money. Rejoice with us. We are putting this cash to good account.'

In the dining-room several courses were served; and wines flowed freely, while preserved fruits and oriental nuts were offered at the conclusion of the meal. The whole was served by two new maids, who were both deft and skilled at their work. Yet I missed Bloomingfield. Where was she? I asked my aunt.

'Bloomingfield is under notice of dismissal,' my aunt informed me, when the room was cleared, and we were alone. 'I could not stand her insolence longer. She overstepped the bounds of her position, and was always carping about money, and the length of hours she was required to be on duty.'

I remembered then that Bloomingfield had indeed been obliged to serve in the house without respite; and I recalled too, her request to Sir Toby that her back wages should be paid. I wondered what was the truth of the matter. But I felt regret that I should not see the dour but trustworthy maid again.

The evening passed pleasantly though I thought sometimes that Sir Toby seemed put out, when Diane mentioned the new improvements to the house. Indeed, before we left, he went into his study and closed the door; as if some matter was displeasing him, and he wished to be alone.

Before we left for Beaufroy House, I went up to my old room, to tidy myself for a moment. As I came down the stairs I saw Diane and Anthony alone by the door to the salon.

They did not touch. They did not speak. There was nothing in their demeanour as they faced one another that could cause any comment, or awake any doubts in even the most insecure mind.

Yet suddenly, a dreadful suspicion assailed me. Suddenly, a fearful doubt and possibility filled my mind.

My two relations were wide apart as I approached them; they turned to me faces both pleasant and kindly; it was clear they had nothing to hide. And yet, it was as if a dark veil had been drawn down over my life; and my whole being was seized with a desolation I had never known before.

And now, time seemed to encapsulate itself. I tried to put from me my fears and suspicions and, as I had planned, I took up my life as the marchioness, and devoted a great deal of time to improving Beaufroy House.

Late spring passed to early summer; time seemed to speed by; yet still my husband and I were apart. We neither of us referred to this. It seemed a forbidden subject, and a prohibited area of our lives.

Yet somehow, gradually, things changed. I noticed suddenly that Anthony did not go out so frequently alone in the evenings; several times now he stayed at home, with me, and we had conversed together on matters concerning the big house; or he had read to me, or we had played cribbage, or another game of cards.

He suddenly seemed to take a new and keener delight in my plans for our home. He was present when the upholsterers arrived; he chose some carpets, he bought oriental rugs. He was unfailingly kind and courteous to me, as he had always been. A deep amity sprang up between us, which gave pleasure to both sides.

We went out several times together now; to various receptions and soirées; and of course I was accorded some respect, due to my new rank as Anthony's wife. Even the Prince Regent was civil, and complimented me upon my *toilette*, and the new way that Mr Percival had arranged my hair. I saw that this pleased Anthony greatly. My success in the social sphere clearly added to his own prestige. In this matter at least I pleased the man I loved so deeply in my secret heart.

It was at Lady Effingham's dinner-party that I observed Diane approach Anthony, and engage him in conversation. I saw that she was displeased, and he tried to disengage himself from her.

Anthony tried to join myself, for I was alone at this particular moment, and awaited his return. As they approached me, her words, uttered in a low but urgent tone, reached my ears.

'... you have not been to see me recently. You are neglecting me, Anthony. What is the matter? What have I done amiss? I am told you spend much time at home now. Heavens above, have I not done enough to earn your consideration and attention?'

When they reached me, Diane said, 'I am chiding your husband, Felicity, for not visiting Toby and myself.' She moved her mother-of-pearl fan, cooling her crimson face. Again, there was nothing to do which any wife could take exception. Again, any suspicions must be ill-based, and rather absurd. 'We will both call upon you shortly, Diane,' I answered, as I laid my hand upon my husband's arm. I saw her notice the gesture, and this, added to the charge of neglect, did not please her.

Later, I was to understand the course of events at this time. I was told that Anthony told a mutual friend, speaking of myself '... her grace, her charm and her abilities please me more than I can say. I am indeed a lucky man to have secured so gifted and pleasant a wife.'

And as for myself, I noticed many admirable qualities in my husband. Far from being a dilettante as regards his military duties, he was a dedicated officer, and wholehearted in his devotion to the Duke of Wellington's cause.

I did not know the precise nature of Anthony's service with the Duke; and he often wore civilian clothes, which puzzled me. But he attended punctiliously at the barracks, and regimental matters took many calls upon his time. Also, he was sometimes absent from home for several days, which I believed entirely were passed on military business, and no doubt about this entered my mind.

So the situation changed for us both. He drew towards me, and I towards him. And the dreadful suspicions which had plagued me before, began to vanish from my mind.

Yet still we were not husband and wife, and I saw no way to remedy this situation. For at this time it was not possible for a wife to discuss with her husband intimate affairs; and for a woman to approach a man with a request for physical love would be unheard of.

Men dominated this society in Regency England. Women had to gain their own way by wiles; but I felt myself not experienced enough to do this; and I dreaded again a rebuff or expression of revulsion. I felt I had suffered enough by my first rejection. I believed my bewildered spirit could accept no more.

So that one night, when I lay in my bed, drowsy with sleep that would not come as I pondered my life and my predicament, when the door of my bedroom opened, I was surprised. I saw that Anthony, in his night clothes and wearing an oriental retiring-gown of maroon silk, had entered the room.

He sat on the edge of the bed, and took me into his arms. I responded to his kiss and caresses of my shoulders and bosom. And so, without a word, he entered my bed, and we began our first night of physical commitment, and the expression of our passion.

This was the first experience for me, of intimate love; of the request to give the body physically and to receive the lover's physical pledging in return. I was moved and enchanted by the experience. The bodily sensation overwhelmed me; but almost more than this, the emotional uplifting of my spirit soothed and comforted the former wounds which had assailed my being and my mind.

I had the feeling also, that for Anthony this was a unique experience. He was not a callow lover; I had not expected that; for in Regency England the men were expected to be fully experienced in these matters; it was the woman whose virginity was prized, and who was expected to come fresh to the sensations of married life.

Yet for Anthony, too, I sensed there was a deeper satisfaction than was normal or expected. He too, seemed overwhelmed by the experience; and this deep and intense pledging of ourselves and our lives to one another.

We slept at last in one another's arms. Dawn

came, and we were still entwined. I awoke with his lips upon mine, and his body again urgent and demanding. And so began my married life, the experience of which I had longed for; and which now seemed to cast a dazzling lustre of satisfaction and felicity over the whole of my future life.

* * *

It was a few days after this, as I sat in the drawing-room alone, busy with some embroidery on the pocket of the retiring-robe which Anthony wore, that Mrs Colgate entered and informed me that a visitor had called for me. I asked her if she had been informed of this lady's name and errand.

'Indeed not, your ladyship. And she is not a lady. She is a person. But she says she is well known to yourself, and that she is sure you will receive her.'

I felt intrigued by this piece of information, and asked Mrs Colgate to show the caller in.

To my surprise, Bloomingfield came into the room. She was dressed all in grey, which matched her hair, and the intense pallor of her skin. She stood before me, civil yet somehow truculent. I saw that she had a great deal on her mind, and I asked her to be seated.

No doubt that she had heard that we had taken on several new staff at Beaufroy House, I told myself, and she had come to offer her services. Her first words took me by surprise.

'I have hesitated over my course of action,' she said, in her rather blunt and brusque way, 'yet I can see no other roads open to me. I feel I must tell you what has occurred.

'I am sorry to hurt you, Miss Felicity, or rather your ladyship. Believe me, I am sincere in that. But this is my only recourse. You will see that this is what I have to do.'

'Have you been dismissed from Rivermead House?' I asked Bloomingfield kindly, for I saw she was in some distress, and I remembered that she had not been sympathetically treated by my former hosts.

'I have left of my own accord, for I could no longer endure the harsh, unfair and unfeeling treatment which was accorded to me.'

She halted. 'No, I must be frank, your ladyship. I have been dismissed without a reference and with much money in back wages owing. Because I spoke out to Lady Diane. I told her what I thought of her behaviour and the plot she hatched and put into operation.'

It was as if a cloud descended upon me at these words; but I did not speak, and waited for Bloomingfield to go on.

'All servants are privy to their masters' concerns, and so was I. I had known what was going on for some time.

'I must tell you that Lord Anthony Lycett and my mistress have been lovers for a long time. There is a back room at Rivermead

House, with its own entrance from a pathway from the Thames. And in this room they met, secretly, unbeknown to Sir Toby, with only myself who observed their assignations and arrangements.

'As you will know, for a considerable period of time, Lord Anthony was impoverished. He had expectations from his uncle, Lord Glenivray, yet his uncle would not allow him a cent of money in advance of his expectations. This was a matter of concern to both Lady Diane and Lord Anthony. They discussed this matter frequently, both in private and in front of myself. I knew well what was going on.'

Through pale lips I forced myself to ask Bloomingfield a question. 'Why did not the Marquis aid his nephew financially?' For this question had earlier occurred to me, and was one of the circumstances surrounding Anthony which had never been made clear. Bloomingfield replied:

'The late Lord Glenivray did not approve of Lord Anthony's way of life. Because Lord Anthony was a rake and a roué.

'He was well known for his conquest of many ladies, even before Lady Diane. He also gambled heavily, engaged in the pursuits of racing and cock-fighting of which his Grace did not approve.

'His Grace also accused his nephew of intransigence concerning his military duties. Lord Anthony had not served overseas, or in the line of battle. The Marquis of Glenivray thought him a coward and a poseur. He did not in any way approve of his nephew's way of life.

'When the Marquis died, only a few months ago, it was found that he had left an unusual will.

'Lord Anthony was his closest relation and stood in line to inherit. Yet the old gentleman decreed that the vast estates should be inherited by his nephew upon one condition only. And if this condition was not complied with as laid down in the will, the entire wealth of the estate should be forfeit, and pass to the benefit of the Crown.

'Of course the Prince Regent knew of this matter, and eagerly awaited the outcome. For although the Prince Regent is amply provided for by the government and Lord Castlereagh, yet he seeks always new ways to finance his dissolute and abandoned way of life.'

I knew that Bloomingfield was speaking the truth, and I was much impressed by her grasp of the situation, and the cogency of her words. I managed to say, 'What were the terms of the late Marquis's will?'

'That Lord Anthony should marry, within three months from the date of the Marquis's death, a young girl of good family, stainless reputation, and a virgin besides,' Bloomingfield replied.

'Needless to say, this was a difficult condition to meet, in Regency England, and in the circles in which Lord Anthony moved.

'Indeed, Lord Anthony was greatly put out by this stipulation, and at a loss as to what to do,' Bloomingfield added. 'But Lady Diane saved the day for him. She proffered to find him a suitable girl, whom he could marry, so that the conditions could be fulfilled. And she hit upon you.

'You were investigated fully, your ladyship. The trustees of this will were strict, and they had the Prince Regent breathing down their necks. But in the space of time allotted to them, they satisfied themselves as to your suitability. And so the marriage was planned. The courtship, such as it was, took place. And you became Lord Anthony Lycett's wife.'

'And it was purely so that he could inherit his uncle's estate, this vast sum of money and the properties,' I said, almost to myself. I heard my voice whisper on the air. 'It was at Diane's instigation, so that he could become a rich man, and take his uncle's place.'

The truth hit me like a physical blow. I felt as if I had been bodily assaulted. 'Leave me please, Bloomingfield,' I said. I felt I had heard enough. I could bear no more. Through a haze of tears I saw the tall, austere figure of the maid leave the room. I heard sobs fall on the air. From a remote and frozen distance, I knew they were my own.

* * *

All the signs had been there for me to see, but I had disregarded them. I could blame my inexperience; yet perhaps also I had not wanted to believe the evidence which had earlier been so clearly presented to my eyes.

I went upstairs to my room, avoiding the servants as I did so. Finally, I allowed my tears, unobstructed, to fall.

Yet finally, I dried my eyes, and my reddened cheeks. I observed myself in my mirror.

So I was just another unremarkable numeral in the social scene of the times, I told myself. As there were cuckolded husbands, so there were deceived wives, and I was one of the latter.

The whole court of the Prince Regent must know the truth about Lady Diane, Anthony and myself. Only I had moved through the charade unaware, and with my eyes blindfolded. I had served my purpose. And my principal purpose must be over.

Again I considered to flee the premises, and return to Pomfret Magna and Aunt Rebecca. Yet I was still, though deceived, a legally married woman, with responsibilities at Beaufroy House, and in my new station in life.

Before, when I had made my decision to remain at Beaufroy House, it seemed to me that I had been vulnerable and untried. But now, I had gained confidence. In myself in my new role as chatelaine of Beaufroy House, and as Anthony Lycett's wife.

Before, I had made my decision from weakness, but now it seemed to me my resolution came from strength. And my earlier decision was suddenly strongly reinforced within me.

I believed that there was some way out of this impasse, but where this was I could not at this moment, see. But some instinct told me not to be precipitate in my actions. To remain steady; not to reveal to anyone that I was aware of Anthony's deceit, and its far-reaching effect upon our lives.

I would take up and continue my life as the Marchioness of Glenivray, and await events. I would bear the fruits of my knowledge alone, and await the indication of the future. But no-one should perceive that now my marriage was to me nothing but a hollow sham.

But my love for Anthony had received a grievous blow, from which, I thought, it would be difficult to rally. And indeed I wondered if my regard for him would ever regain the force and depth I had felt for him before; or my reliance upon him and joy in his presence be recreated.

CHAPTER EIGHT

And so, time sped by. The war between England and France and her allies continued, and life at Beaufroy House pursued its by now well-regulated course.

In February of this year 1814, the Duke of Wellington's spring run had begun. The Duke had miraculously transformed his band of scum and his infamous rabble into a finely disciplined and highly competent fighting force. He was revered by his men; and to his soldiers he gave a respect and appreciation uncommon for the times.

Yet in spite of the seemingly smooth course of military events, the tension was not eased in England, and certainly not among the fighting forces. It was as if the Duke did not believe his victories would continue; and was guarding against an unexpected or unforeseen reverse.

And then later this year, a strange incident took place; and two people entered my existence with impact, and with unforeseeable effect upon my future and my life.

I had been shopping in an area called Bond Street, when, as I returned to Beaufroy House in the carriage, I saw another carriage drawn up outside the house, and two strangers alighting from the vehicle.

This was an old and shabby conveyance, so unlike the one Anthony now maintained; and its two occupants were bizarre in appearance, and seemed most unlikely as social callers at Beaufroy House. I watched this pair with interest, as they mounted the steps towards the front door.

The man was a mendicant, that was plain to see. He was dressed almost in rags, and in filthy rags, too. The woman was also dressed as a female beggar; one of that unfortunate band forced to tread roads in search of shelter and sustenance. I watched them as they halted at the top of the steps, before the door.

Yet there was something in the woman's stance which was out of place to her garb. Her bearing was very erect; almost queenly. Her attitude as she glanced around her was critical, even imperious. She gave the impression that she expected others to do her bidding; and not the reverse.

They have made a mistake, I thought. Old Benjamin will turn them away. But to my surprise I saw the door open, and the two strangers entered the hall.

I followed the two visitors, deep in thought. In the hallway, I found that the woman had vanished, but the young man was seated in an antique brocade chair, easing his worn boots off his feet. He looked at me with surprise, and rose to his feet.

I saw now, that in spite of the dilapidation of his appearance, this young man was personable, and even handsome. He was clearly auburn in colouring, yet with dark eyes and brows. His skin, beneath the mud and grime, I could see was clear and fresh in colour. He smiled tentatively, his lips parting over even teeth.

'Is there something this household can do for you, sir?' I asked the stranger. 'Benjamin has admitted you, and will be, I am sure, glad to provide you with a meal and facilities for washing.

'We help those whom we are able,' I continued. 'We ask only that they will call at Beaufroy House by the back door. The servants' hall is there, and Mrs Colgate, our housekeeper, keeps a stock of food for needy callers. We try not to turn those who deserve our clemency, away.'

I saw surprise flash into the young man's eyes, but before he could reply, Anthony entered the hall from the rear study. He hastened to the young man's side.

'Paul!' he cried. 'So you have arrived safely; and your mission is accomplished. Thank God you are both safe!' And so saying my husband clasped the stranger in his arms, and both stood, as if expressing relief at the end of some long anxiety or period of strain. They drew apart, and then saluted, as if they were on a parade ground, or in the execution of some military orders. Anthony continued to speak to the stranger.

'The Countess is resting in the salon. Come, get cleaned off, and we will take food and wine!' And then Anthony realized that I was standing motionless nearby, watching the surprising scene. A look of contrition passed over his face.

'Forgive me my dear, this matter in hand is so pressing, I forgot the civilities. Felicity, please allow me to present my cousin, Paul Lycett, recently arrived from France. And Paul, congratulate me please, for this is Felicity, my wife.'

Both Paul Lycett and I murmured the pleasantries of the time. Yet I saw the amazement upon Paul's face, as he realized that Anthony had married, and that before him was his cousin's new wife.

He looked at me keenly, and I also returned the gaze. And yet somehow, in some indefinable way, our glance of explorations lost its edge. Our surprise was mutual, but so was our interest. We looked away, and yet some indescribable communication had passed between us. And a strange awareness of one another had been born.

Benjamin now came for Paul Lycett, to take him upstairs and attend him during his toilet. I saw the white towels over the old man's arm, and saw a maid precede the two men with a jug and bowl of water. Mrs Colgate entered the salon, no doubt to see and attend the new lady visitor. But before I too could enter the big room, Anthony laid a hand upon my arm, and drew me along the hallway to the book-lined study.

He bade me take off my cloak and hat, and be seated. I did so, as he poured us both a glass of wine.

'And now I must reveal to you information which has been secret and hidden until now,' Anthony began. 'Perhaps you will have wondered about certain aspects of my life. But now, I will reveal the inner core of some mysteries. Listen Felicity, for the outcome of Paul's last mission vitally concerns us both.

'You will know that I am a serving soldier attached to the Duke of Wellington's headquarters in London. I know you have wondered at my lack of military engagements, and that often I am not in uniform, and appear to be footloose and feckless in the direction of my life.'

He paused. 'You must know that the Duke of Wellington is a gifted and skilled military commander, who leaves nothing to chance. He believes that preceding all military endeavours, information must clear the way. He is adamant that his intelligence service supply him with accurate and up to the minute details concerning all aspects of the enemy's plans and suggested campaigns. He is a stickler for precise advance knowledge before he makes a move.

'Yes Felicity, and for this he has employed serving soldiers as agents in the field. Yes, they are spies, yet in service of their country there is no dishonour in this designation. This corps of agents has served the Duke well, until now... A serious complication has arisen, and one which threatens the Duke's plans and indeed the success of the British armies in their next venture against their enemies, the French.'

Anthony paused, then continued. 'There is a serious leakage of information concerning the corps of agents, to the French high command. Many of these agents, gifted and dedicated men, have been apprehended by the French forces, arrested and thrown into jail. In many cases they have been tortured, and have not survived.

'The Duke has given orders that this present corps of agents must be withdrawn, and the procedures scrutinized, with the intention of discovering the leakage of information. He gave orders that certain trusted men of his London headquarters must go into France, in disguise, to alert the agents there, and to escort them home.

'I have been one of the men entrusted with this work, and so has my cousin, Paul Lycett. We have been successful in our efforts so far; in that we have located several of the endangered agents, and have managed to bring them back to England. And have ourselves evaded capture and death.'

I was astounded by this information from my husband, and I cried, 'Why did you not inform me of these matters before? I have been kept in ignorance of your duties with the Duke, and the dangers you have faced and undergone.

'Surely you could have shared your

problems with me? I could have aided you. I would have regarded it as an honour to have been associated with you in your aims and effort for our country, and the Duke.'

Anthony rose to his feet, and crossed to my side. He took my hand in his and raised it to his lips. 'I could not bear to bring you into this darker side of my existence. I wanted to spare you anxiety and pain.

'Oh, I know you long to experience everything life has to offer. In our moments of passion you told me fully of your longings and desires! But I did not wish to be the one to bring you emotions of doubt or despair. There is enough adversity in life without our inflicting these circumstances upon one another.'

I rose to my feet and faced Anthony. I spoke with great sincerity and earnestness.

'But what can I do now, now that I know the truth? Please tell me, I want to aid you in what you are engaged upon, at this moment.'

Anthony said, 'Paul was despatched to France to bring back to London an agent called Charles Latham. The London headquarters learned that he was in danger, and was hiding in an apartment in Paris near to the site of the former bastille.

'But when Paul arrived, he found that Charles Latham was wounded and was too ill to be moved to England. He was in danger of discovery in Paris, so his fiancée, the Countess de Courcy—in whose apartment he was lodged—offered him accommodation in her château on a tributary of the Seine.

'Charles then asked, nay demanded, that his fiancée should be taken to London in his place.

'As he was an extremely valuable agent, and indeed, the head of the corps, this request was considered by the *chef de mission*, in Paris.

'Permission was granted, and Paul also agreed to this course. For the safety of the countess was also at risk. And she too needed to escape from those who threatened both Charles and herself.

'As you will have seen, these two have now arrived in London,' Anthony continued. 'The lady now in our house is a French woman of high birth, the Countess de Courcy. If you wish to aid us, Felicity, I beg you to attend her, make her welcome, and keep her hidden here.

'I cannot tell you of the importance of this, since we know that there are French agents infiltrated into the services in London.

'And the French must not find Charles. For he carries with him much security information of great value to both sides. He is a key man in the Duke of Wellington's strategy. And he must be kept in hiding until another mission can bring him out.'

Anthony paused. 'Your immediate task, my dear, is to make the countess welcome, to comfort and encourage her. And keep her presence a secret. Beyond this request, I cannot, at the moment, afford to go.'

*　　*　　*

There was a room upstairs which was kept exclusively for the use of women guests to Beaufroy House, and it was to this chamber that I hastened with all speed.

I found the countess was being attended by Mrs Colgate, and had just stepped out of a bath of hot and soapy water. She stood on the bathing-mat, wrapped in a huge white towel. I looked at her with interest, and so she observed myself.

I saw that she was tall and thin, but that her figure had a ripe development, unusual in a young woman. Her hair was black, and hung freely to her wet shoulders, in damp curls. Her complexion was olive, her colour rather high and well defined. Her eyes were black also, and they shone now with a rather fierce and penetrating light.

'You must be the marchioness,' she said to me in a clear voice, speaking English, and almost without a French accent. 'I am Louisa, Countess de Courcy. My family is an ancient one in France, and my father was connected to the Court of Louis.' Her tone was brusque, almost defiant, I thought. I acknowledged the pleasantries and crossed to her side. I began to gather up the filthy rags she had shed, from the floor.

'I shall require a complete new wardrobe, from tomorrow,' the countess told me. 'Several dresses of brocade and velvet, and underwear of silk. No cambric. No linen. Silk only. And hose of fine knit also, and garters of satin.

'Paul has promised me these things. He told me that your husband is a wealthy man, and can well afford to provide the wardrobe I left behind in France.' She scrutinized my outdoor dress, and the cape which I still wore around my shoulders. 'English fashion is a bore,' she said. 'But English garments must suffice for the present time.'

I felt extremely put out by the countess's brusqueness and presumption. But before I could make any reply she went on:

'And of course I shall require my own personal maid. I trust you will put at my disposal a servant to be under my direction entirely. And someone young,' she added. 'I do not like aged people about me.' She glanced disparagingly at the devoted and revered Mrs Colgate, and I saw the old servitor stiffen.

'I will see what I can do,' I answered coolly. 'And of course Mrs Colgate will not attend you. Mrs Colgate is too high in rank in this household to be a personal maid. She is here to aid you at the present moment only as a favour to you and to myself.'

The countess did not reply, but I knew she accepted the reproof. She said, 'Be that as it may, but I require clothing here and now. I trust you will make available to me some garments from your own supply.'

I had already decided that this must be my course, but to be told so by this unpredictable guest did not please me. However, I remembered Anthony's request to me, and I went to my room, and returned with several dresses over my arm. I hoped that the countess would make a choice, and that I could take the remainder of the garments back to their hangers in my cupboard. But she seized the whole supply. And tossed the expensive garments in a heap beside the bed.

'The evening dinner will be served in the dining-room at six o'clock,' I told this capricious young woman. 'Mrs Colgate will conduct you there, when you are ready.'

'I shall not dine in public this evening,' the countess told me. 'I shall require a meal served in my room. With wine,' she added. 'I do not trust English water. It is notorious for giving one the...' She used an unprintable word which meant looseness of the bowels. I thought her behaviour strange for one who continually stressed her high degree.

I changed swiftly for the evening meal, and went down to the dining-room. The two men present rose to their feet as I entered the room.

I saw that now that Paul had bathed and changed from the rags of his mendicant's disguise, he was of attractive aspect indeed; his face was handsome, and his bearing easy and polished.

He was not so tall as Anthony, but was

broader in the shoulders and limbs. There was about him an aura of strength, and also competence, as if he was skilled in many practical matters; and would not be outfaced by any adverse circumstance, or difficult assignment encountered in his life or career.

Both Anthony and Paul made themselves exceedingly pleasant to me; as if their discussions were over, and they wished to put grave matters aside. Hardly had we begun the meal, when the door of the room opened, and the countess came in.

I saw that she had done her hair in the French way, mounted as a pompadour on the top of her head. She wore one of my best dresses, the one of blue silk, with a bodice of brocade. I saw to my dismay that the countess had cut the bodice with scissors to make the *décolletage* lower, and had ripped off a beading of small pearls. The dress was clearly damaged beyond repair. Yet she did not appear aware, or contrite.

'I changed my mind,' she said. 'I decided to dine *en famille*, after all.' She took the place indicated by Anthony, and Benjamin hastily brought her cover-plate and viands. Her glance upon us all was friendly and composed. She was harmless as a lamb, her demeanour said. She wished no-one any harm, and was a docile and grateful guest.

Indeed, during the meal she said to me, 'No doubt you are wondering as to my presence in

England since I am a French national, and bear an honoured French name.

'But my mother was English, and I received some education in England, at an academy near Bath.

'I admire English institutions and English manners and customs. Indeed, I adore the English way of life, and English people. And truly, I have shown this preference by being engaged to an Englishman!'

A shadow passed over her face. 'I think constantly of Charles, and am desolated to have left him behind in France. Yet he insisted, and the Duke of Wellington sent me a personal message to flee. I was in danger from the French. My own countrymen! For my British sympathies were known and condemned. I am glad indeed to have escaped, and thank you all for your clemency.'

Louisa de Courcy's eyes upon us were grateful and guileless. I could see that the men were impressed. But I gazed at her with wonder and surprise. And kept my own secret conclusions to myself.

CHAPTER NINE

And now a circumstance took place, which caused me some distress. Sir Toby Bullough fell ill from a pox which was currently sweeping through London.

I visited him on behalf of Anthony and myself, and took him some comforts and remembrances. He seemed grateful for these attentions, and took my hand in his with warmth and affection. I felt grieved to see the man who had always treated me so kindly laid low in this way.

To my surprise, my Aunt Diane received me with a lack of enthusiasm on my visits; indeed, she seemed indifferent to me, and sometimes even hostile.

She questioned me as to my social activities with Anthony. Whose receptions had we attended; whose houses visited; who had called upon us; had we entertained? I answered her as civilly and as fully as I could. But I felt at a loss as to the trend of her enquiries. And wondered at the malice evident in her concern.

Whereas before, she had seemed eager for me to marry Anthony—but for Anthony to gain his coveted end, no less! But now she seemed to view the marriage with disfavour; and I certainly found no approval in her eyes.

At this time, I noticed also a further change in the attitude of Anthony, my husband, to myself. I had noticed earlier that he had spent much more time at Beaufroy House; and had not so frequently visited London entertainments alone. But now, it was almost as if a period of courtship was taking place between Anthony and myself.

He seemed to woo me ardently; bringing me presents of jewellery and gifts of china and statuary. He showered upon me the fruits of his inheritance, offering me dresses, cloaks and kid pumps in abundance. I wondered greatly at this change of attitude; this reversal of feelings in his heart.

For during the days of our courtship I had felt him less than ardent; he had been a reluctant pursuer, bound only to his course by the vista of immense wealth at the end of the pursuit. But now ... It was as if he had truly fallen in love with myself. As if he had at last found the counterpart of the secret image he had carried in his heart.

The countess noticed Anthony's attentions and concern for me. 'He is besotted with you, or becoming that way,' she said, with a curl of her well-defined lips. 'But Englishmen are all or nothing. It is their nature. Their affections alter like the wind. He can just as soon fall out of love with you, as into love with you. As for myself, I have this strange power over men. I cannot understand it, but it has always been that way.'

I noticed that she fluttered her eyelashes and smiled beguilingly at Anthony and Paul; but so far they had not responded to her advances.

For my own part, I found it difficult to respond to Anthony's change of heart. My hurt had been so deep and intense concerning his deception of me, it was difficult indeed to assume the role of a flattered wife. I found that my affections towards him were not kindled; and my pain and scepticism remained.

Imperceptibly, Sir Toby's condition deteriorated. He lay in his bed wasted and ravaged with pain. On one occasion when I sat by his bedside, he took my hand in his own.

'I have loved her so ardently,' he said. 'I have adored Diane. She has been the lodestar of my life.'

'I know of your deep affection,' I said. 'And I honour you for it, as does the rest of the world.'

'I have had so little to offer her,' he continued. 'No wealth. No high position. Even my service at the Ministry, as keeper of the archives to the Duke of Wellington, has been in a minor capacity. Yet I have longed to give her so much. She could have worn some high estate, like a crown.'

He fell asleep, and Paul sponged his lips with brandy. For Paul had accompanied me to visit my Aunt Diane and Sir Toby; and his firm and sincere presence had helped me during the visit, and had seemed to bring some peace to Sir Toby, too.

'When will you return to France?' I asked Paul, in the carriage as we left Rivermead House. For I knew that soon Paul must leave us; his service with the Duke would call him away from the safety of Beaufroy House.

'The Duke has instructed that another

agent, David Exeter, should journey to France, to try to bring out Charles Latham,' he told me. 'I await the outcome of this assignment. If it does not succeed, I shall be pressed into service again. For I know the territory, and the business of disguise and concealment. And the escape-route also is known to me, for I have travelled this route many times.'

It was during this period that I was presented at court, to their majesties King George and Queen Charlotte. The King was having one of his more lucid intervals, and he engaged me in pleasant conversation about the necessity for the correct feeding of livestock—for I found he had a great interest in husbandry and the countryside.

The Queen for her part, gave me a monologue on the upbringing of children, upon which she was an expert. She eyed me in a friendly yet meaningful way, as if she was giving me an overt hint to start a family, and produce my first child. She clearly thought she was giving me instruction that would be useful when I at last bore Anthony his first child, and became a mother myself.

It was at this reception that a curious incident occurred. My Aunt Diane was presented, but without Sir Toby, of course. During the evening I saw her chatting animatedly with her friends; it was while she was so engaged, that I observed a man approach her.

I saw my aunt's surprise as he addressed her, and I instantly realized that the new arrival was the same man whom I had seen in the hallway of Rivermead House, calling upon Sir Toby.

Clearly, he was an unwelcome newcomer to Diane; yet he was plainly asking that he might have converse with her. I watched them walk away onto the terrace of the palace, together.

Later, when I saw this man alone, I asked Anthony his identity. 'He is a professional diplomat, a counsellor to the ambassador of Belgium, well known in London society. His name is Leopold Vaes. But do not interest yourself in him, my dear, for he is not to your taste in any way.

'He frequents only male clubs, such as Bucks and Blades. And his main interest in life is the game of chess!'

When we arrived home, following this soirée, it was to find Louisa de Courcy awaiting for us in a state of sulks.

'Why was I not included in this invitation?' she cried. 'You stole off and left me alone. Paul has been at the barracks, and I have no-one to amuse me.

'You could have presented me to your king and queen, and I hear the Prince Regent loves ladies. Why have I been denied admittance to London society? I regard this as an insult and a slight.'

In vain we tried to explain to her the necessity that she remain hidden in our house.

'It is by the Duke of Wellington's clemency alone that you escaped from France, and are being kept secure in England,' Anthony assured her.

'Do you not know there are agents in London who would love to know your whereabouts. They could take you hostage, and through intimidation gain knowledge of the hiding-place of Charles Latham.'

'Please gain some sense, Louisa. Do not tempt fate. Conditions concerning the agents are serious enough, without your adding further to the trouble and dislocation.'

She left us with ill grace. She seemed to lack even basic understanding of her condition, and the efforts being made on her behalf.

There was an open space at the back of Beaufroy House, which was grassed over, providing a lawn and a garden of shrubs and small trees. I often walked there, and Paul also loved to stroll in this green and pleasant, though private and enclosed space.

Here he flew the falcons he loved; there were stables for the horses, and these he helped to groom. For these occasions he wore the clothes of a working man; long moleskin trousers and a jerkin of brown leather. He wore sabots upon his feet and was not afraid of grime and grease upon his hands.

He smiled at my unspoken observation of himself and his pursuits. 'I am a trained wheelwright,' he said. 'And a blacksmith and forester. I was brought up in the country upon the estate of a second cousin, for I am an orphan, without other family. I early learned country skills, and these I love, and they have never left me.'

He showed me then how to replace the wheel of the carriage which had become dislocated from its iron staple. I admired his dedication, and the breadth and direction of his life.

For between Paul and myself a close friendship had sprung up. He was very perceptive; he appeared to know the hidden circumstances behind many situations and circumstances at Beaufroy House.

To speak to him on these terms of undemanding friendship was a great comfort to me; and often a help when I felt perplexed by the circumstances of my life, and the strange way things had developed.

He spoke no words of intimacy, he did not hint at, or reveal his inner knowledge. But his presence gave me a sensation of support and strength, upon which I grew to rely more and more as time went on.

Anthony had left Beaufroy House for a few days, travelling on one of his assignments for the Duke. I had said goodbye to him without a qualm, not knowing when he would return. In his absence, Paul had assumed his place as head of the household. He wore his command lightly, yet his authority was firm and definite, though not overtly revealed.

I began to dread when Paul would be called for further service overseas. 'When will you depart?' I pressed him again, as we strolled in the garden one day. 'Very shortly, I am afraid,' he answered, and his regret sounded genuine; he seemed this time deeply reluctant to go.

'Rumours abound,' he continued. 'Some say Napoleon is threatening to abdicate, and certainly the Duke of Wellington has been received with acclaim in Paris.

'The Duke appears bland during the paeons of praise heaped upon him. But beneath his exterior, he is a dedicated soldier still. And he insists upon the dedication of all ranks of his forces in exchange for his own.

'David Exeter has returned to England without Charles Latham,' Paul resumed. 'Another agent, already in France, called William Lansbury, has been instructed to take his place, and to continue to search for Charles. I am ordered to keep on the alert, and to be ready for service overseas at any time.'

'Let me aid you in your preparations,' I offered eagerly. 'I can sew, launder garments, do anything you require to prepare you for your next mission.'

'I would appreciate some sewing,' Paul answered. 'For though I often travel as a beggar or ostler, yet my garments must also conceal badges of identity and the tools of my trade.

'For I have to be prison breaker,' he said. 'I

have to be able to defend myself in combat, and must carry a weapon. The details of documents I can carry in my head. Specifications, troop movements, details of armaments, deployment of agents and counter agents, all these I can remember as if reading from a page! But I must have hidden pockets to carry my tools. Can you aid me? Can you prepare secret caches within my mendicant's robes?'

I went to work with a will, doing all possible to aid my new friend. He was not effusive in his thanks; that was not his way. He was not so polished and free with words, as Anthony was. Yet his gratitude was apparent, and he gave me a small locket of enamel and pearls, which he had gained during his travels in France.

At the end of this week, Anthony returned home, and the next day Sir Toby Bullough died.

* * *

We all attended the funeral. Though not dominating and strident in his life, yet Sir Toby had gained a wide circle of friends, and was clearly highly regarded by a cross section of London society.

Many friends from the Duke of Wellington's headquarters attended the funeral; acquaintances from his social life, relations, and friends of Diane's. All sincerely mourned this man who had been a devoted friend to many. Asking nothing in return; seeking only to give his interest and company to those whom he met, and admired.

I felt stricken by the passing of Sir Toby, who had shown me only kindness and consideration since I had arrived in London, and when I had entered his house. I thought that without him, my life at Rivermead House would have been bleak indeed.

Diane was robed entirely in black, with a veil, as was the custom of widows at this time. Yet even this garb could not quell her beauty; and her regal carriage and vivid colouring were set off by the sombre garments, rather than quenched by sobriety of the occasion, and her mourning.

Some instinct, I knew not why, made me glance around to see if Sir Toby's friend, the Belgian counsellor with whom he had played chess, was present in the Richmond church. But I could not see his tall and fashionable form. But I knew my eyes were blurred with tears; and the diplomat may have been present, though unobserved by myself.

All the congregation watched Diane lead the cortège from the church, towards the burial ground. Again she moved in queenly fashion, her attitude composed and in command of herself.

Yet she now faces great changes in her life, I told myself, as Anthony and I joined the family mourners behind the widowed wife. But how great the changes were, and the events they would lead to, I did not know. But I was very soon to find out.

CHAPTER TEN

It was a short time after Sir Toby's funeral, that I fell ill with a slight chill of the bones. Yet I thought it expedient to keep on my feet and to move around, and I carried on with the activities of my life, as usual.

I had made arrangements to attend an afternoon reception given by the wife of a member of the diplomatic circle at the court. I had dressed for this, and had even said goodbye to Anthony before he left the house, arranging to meet him for the evening meal, on my return.

Yet on the point of venturing out, I felt the aches quicken in my limbs, and knew I could not sustain an afternoon of polite socializing and formal behaviour. I then repaired to the salon to rest on a *chaise-longue*, while Benjamin was despatched to my hostess with formal apologies and regrets.

There was a small room opening off the salon called the book-room. This was not the study proper, which was a vast room filled with leather-tooled books and marble busts of bygone scholars. In this minute chamber were kept volumes of instruction on estate management, housewifery, etiquette, and the various crafts which made up a wealthy family's life.

I had entered this tiny room to find myself a book to pass the restful hours, when I heard the door of the salon open, and two people entered the room. Almost immediately I heard voices.

'I have asked to see you, because the matter is now urgent, and needs attention. I know you have been avoiding me, and I am at a loss to explain this. But the bonds between us are too firm and of too long-standing to be lightly severed. You must hear what I have to say.'

'I welcome you to my home, Diane,' I heard Anthony reply. 'And I shall hear what you have to say with interest. But no good cause will be served by a belligerent attitude. Please speak in a civil way, and so, I will reply.'

'I have tried soft speaking to you, and it has brought no result. And now I must speak frankly, with all dice thrown on the table.' Diane paused. 'I am asking, nay insisting, that the conditions of the pact between us, made formerly, should be fulfilled and honoured in every particular.'

'This pact as you call it,' said Anthony, 'was made in the past. But the present has altered everything for me. I consider that I have discharged my obligations to you, in full. And need be asked to do no more.'

'Not so,' answered Diane. 'You are a man of

honour and must fulfil the responsibilities of your solemnly given word.'

'I paid you the sum of money you requested for your services to me in this matter you mention,' Anthony replied. 'You expressed yourself as satisfied. What more do you want? Surely the payment of this large sum of money ended all obligations between us?'

'The sum of money you paid me for procuring Felicity from the country for you was spent, as you know, upon improvements to Rivermead House. But now that Toby is dead, I find myself in reduced straits. I ask for more. And I ask also that the further condition implicit in our earlier relationship, should be fulfilled.'

'Diane, it is true I loved you earlier,' Anthony countered, 'and I appreciated your action in bringing Felicity, my wife, from the country, and enabling me to fulfil the requirements of my late uncle's will, and so please the trustees and inherit his estate. But now, cannot you see, for us to resume any close relationship would be impossible?

'Indeed, I have no wish to deceive Felicity in this way. Nothing is further from my thoughts. She deserves the best I can give, and this I am determined to grant her.'

'You have changed your tune,' Diane said. 'Before, you agreed to take out a bill of divorcement from her, as soon as was decent, when the money and estates were in your hands.

'And I also pledged myself to seek annulment of my marriage to Toby, which I could well have done, for our union had not been consummated for some time. And a termination of our marriage was logical, and indeed inevitable.

'Then we were to be free to marry. Then you promised to make me your wife. You know this is the truth. This was your pledge. Given to me to persuade me to procure Felicity to be your wife.

'And now that Toby is dead—the way is open to us without let or hindrance to our plans. Only Felicity stands in the way, but that is a problem you can easily solve.'

'It is true there was closeness between us at that time,' Anthony conceded grudgingly. 'But in the heat of passion one can make pledges difficult, later, to fulfil.

'Do not forget your own anxiety to aid me,' Anthony continued. 'You loved me then. If you loved me now you would not pursue this matter so ardently, but would grant me my release from an impossible pledge. Love is not truly love that seeks to take the other's passion by force.'

'You are skilled in words, Anthony Lycett,' Diane cried. 'Remember how eagerly you wooed me, and persuaded me to deceive Toby. But now is the reality. And now I insist on the fulfilment of obligations. You must divorce

Felicity and send her away, out of your life.'

'I will not do that. I will not divorce her,' Anthony countered vehemently. 'It would break her heart and ruin my own life.'

'At the very least despatch her away into the country, and if you will not marry me, let us have a regularized relationship such as the Prince Regent has with Mrs Fitzherbert,' Diane said.

'You know that now, since the Prince has honoured Mrs Fitzherbert with cohabitation, this type of alliance has become fashionable, and is accepted by the court as almost as legal as the relationship between man and wife.'

'I do not propose to do any such thing,' Anthony answered, and his distaste was revealed in his voice.

'Am I to believe that this is your final word?'

'You may take it as my final word. I do not wish to discuss this matter again, and my mind is quite made up. I consider you were amply repaid for your services to me, and I have no intention of taking legal action to enable me to make you my wife. Or my legalized mistress in the eyes of the court.'

'Yet this is not the last and final verdict,' Diane replied, and I heard the vehemence and malice in her voice. 'I hold the cards, you will hear further in this matter, from me.

'The situation is not finalized, Anthony Lycett. Perhaps you and your bride will live to rue the day you refused to honour your pledge.

For I am not one to take insolence lightly, nor to accept being put down...

'Wait. You will see. Your behaviour will be repaid. And you will live to regret your cruelty, and the bonds of honour you have scorned and not fulfilled.'

I heard then the swish of silken skirts, and the sound of footsteps upon the carpet of the salon. I heard the door open, then close, softly. And now, there was silence in the deserted room.

* * *

I sat quite still in the book-room, with a volume upon the arts of smocking and quilting motionless upon my lap. Finally, I rose to my feet and crossed the small room, to look out on the paved courtyard, outside.

But of course I had known for some time, earlier events had fully revealed to me that Anthony had married me in order to fulfil the conditions of his late uncle's will, and so to gain his uncle's monies and estates.

I accepted that the marriage had been loveless on his side. Upon mine, it had been as a dream come true; an event of ecstatic proportions that had dwarfed everything that had gone before in my life.

But I knew now that there had been a further, hidden clause in the arrangement between Diane and Anthony. That I was to be dismissed by a bill of divorcement after the money and estates had been received. Divorced or despatched to the country, at any rate robbed of my marriage, my status, my chance of happiness, and my place at my husband's side.

How small a step it is, I thought, from innocence to disillusionment! I pondered further the circumstances now impinging upon my life.

I realized, I believed now, that Anthony had intended to fulfil his stated obligations to Diane but that somehow, in some way, my presence with him, and my proximity in his life, had altered his intention.

I remembered the rapture of our first night together; the amity which had later come about.

There was no doubt that from acceptance, or even indifference, Anthony had begun to care for me, even to love me in his own way. All the signs of our life together showed me that. And yet...

We had continued our intimate life together as man and wife, following our first experience of the emotions which had assailed us, when we had first come together.

Yet he had made but few demands upon me, I was surprised to discover. I thought often that he visited the professional courtesans on the fringes of the court for the relief of his desires; or consorted with certain ladies close to the Prince Regent who, it was said, were free with their favours, and yielded frequently to men of rank or consequence, attached to the royal circle.

I believed that this had been Anthony's custom before our marriage—even when he was the lover of Diane. And I felt sure that he continued this habit and inclination, even though we were married, and he had found pleasure in our making love, and our proximity during the long hours of the night.

Some instinct, deeply embedded within me, told me that this was a generality among men at this time. That wife and mistress were kept apart, but both enjoyed. I realized that all around me other women were doing this; accepting, yet trying to hold on to their marriages and their love. This is a harsh and licentious age, I thought. And without pity for the weaker members of both sexes.

Yet there was no doubt that again my love had received yet another blow; another grievous hurt had been added to my disillusion of before. It was as if the will to carry on, to continue with the charade of my marriage, was being sapped from me. Only the determination to survive remained.

And yet this is what I must do, I told myself. Survive. I steeled myself and called up all my strength and resolution. I must hold my head high and defy the world, and outface the customs of the court and our immediate circle.

This was my only weapon—my own courage placed like a shield before the world. To take refuge in histrionics, accusations and reproaches would be to reveal a fatal weakness. I could only fight the condition of the time with my own weapons and armour. I had no choice but to make the best effort I could, and hope for success.

I climbed the stairs to my room, still in my formal dress for attending the afternoon reception, which now must be almost over. To my surprise, I found Louisa de Courcy sitting in a bend of the staircase, hunched in a ball, with her head hidden in her arms. I was greatly surprised to find her there, and in this distraught condition.

'Why Louisa,' I cried. 'What is the matter? Have you been taken ill? Come with me, into my room, and I will find the camphor. You can rest on my *chaise*, and Mrs Colgate will bring us an infusion of tea.'

I helped the trembling girl up the stairs, and into my bedchamber. She sat down and I looked at her tear-stained face.

'I cannot bear it here, any longer, in London,' she told me. 'It is cold and dark and dreary. When I look from the windows I see only streets, and carriages, and stones and walls, with no trees. And this house is cold. I cannot get warm. And my bed is a mattress, not feathers. And you give me no cognac, I am used to cognac, I cannot bear this dry sack, and ale and fermented wines.'

'I am sorry,' I answered. 'I did not realize that you were not comfortable here. It was remiss of me. I apologize.'

I was suddenly contrite, thinking that although this guest was troublesome and fault-finding, yet I had somehow neglected her comfort and welfare. She continued;

'I long to see Charles. Time is passing by, and I hear no word. It was wrong of me to come to England. I should have stayed in France, by his side.

'And I am a prisoner here. A prisoner! No-one takes me anywhere. I am cooped up, day after day, with only my own thoughts for company.'

This was not strictly true, I thought, since I had sought Louisa out frequently, and had tried to involve her in matters concerning the house. And both Anthony and Paul had been civil and kindly to her, while ignoring her advances for flirtation. Her ennui was largely her own fault, I decided. She had no inner reserves, and no resolution to solve her own problems.

'But how can we take you into English society?' I answered her. 'You are a French national, bearing an ancient French name. And England is at war with France. On the continent a bitter conflict is continuing between the two countries. It is not possible for you to venture from this house. You are here for your own protection. Surely you realize that.'

'So you say,' Louisa answered sulkily. 'But I think the Duke of Wellington is keeping me a prisoner here. What efforts is the Duke making to bring Charles back to England? Why has my fiancé not appeared? I am tired of this situation, I can tell you. And I am pondering how to bring some end to this stalemate in my affairs.'

Mrs Colgate entered with tea, and I helped Louisa to compose herself. I myself sponged her face, and then she applied the elaborate cosmetics she used, and rearranged the raven dark pyramid of her hair. Inconsequentially, when we were alone, she began to talk to me again.

'I cannot describe to you the disorder and confusion of life in France at the present time. Not only from this devastating war, but from the legacy of revolution and unrest which has swept through my country in recent years.

'The revolution with its guillotine and bastille horrified many of my countrymen. Men and women were slaughtered wholesale, and not only aristocrats, but anyone who offended the self-styled rulers of my country. The best seemed to go. The revolution left France leaderless, and in the hands of the self-seekers and the corrupt.

'And even now, in civilian gaols, prisoners are tortured with ancient weapons of torture.

Women are not spared...' Louisa turned to me a face ashen in hue; her eyes were dilated and her hands clenched. She began to recount to me, in detail, some of the bestial and obscene acts which were perpetrated against the inhabitants of French gaols. Her voice broke, and again she dissolved into tears.

'But Louisa,' I cried. 'The revolution is over. It has been over for some time. And the tortures you describe took place during the inquisition, surely? And the inquisition is ended, too.'

I waited for her to reply, and she said, 'Both the revolution and the inquisition may be over, in name, but their shadows remain. They are not over in reality.

'In some parts of Paris the guillotine is still in use. Prisoners are transported to their deaths in tumbrils, even as they were at the revolution.

'And the tortures... They continue. French gaolers learnt the Spanish methods well, and still apply them. I weep for my country, Felicity. I weep and mourn for the happy days which are gone and past.'

I felt greatly affected by this speech of Louisa's. She had spoken cogently and rationally, yet with deep emotion. Her words were not those of an hysterical girl, as they had been previously. I marvelled again at the many sides of her nature; she was like a diamond whose facets give off light with every movement. Again I soothed her and helped her to her feet.

I had to steel myself to go downstairs for the evening meal, and to hide the grievous thoughts within my mind; and the dreadful pall of pain which had filled my heart, concerning my own affairs.

But as we sat within the salon, taking a glass of wine before old Benjamin announced the repast, I took Paul into my confidence concerning Louisa, and asked him to aid her to recover from her present downcast state of mind.

So after the evening dinner, Paul began to try to teach Louisa how to play chess. They sat with the board on a small table between them, and soon their pleasant voices rang through the salon, as Paul described the moves, and Louisa tried to master them.

I observed them with a smile, seeing their two heads close together, and their hands often touching as they moved the pieces.

They made a striking and fitting couple, I told myself. Paul of russet hue, and Louisa raven dark. I saw that Louisa had now begun to flirt with Paul, eyeing him coquettishly, and asking him provoking personal questions. She flaunted herself like a peacock for his approval. I saw the gleam of amusement in Paul's eyes.

I marvelled again at the duality of this beautiful young woman, who in one moment could weep for her vanished lover; and the next could flirt outrageously with another man.

I did not know that her intransigence and vanity were to have serious effects upon us all in the future. And that her strange arrogance was to endanger our lives; was to take us to the brink of disaster. And beyond.

CHAPTER ELEVEN

A few days after the previous events, I was sitting sewing a small pouch for Paul to take on his travels, when Mrs Colgate entered the room, and informed me that Lady Diane Bullough had called to see me.

I was in the small sitting-room at the rear of the house; an intimate chamber which the whole family often preferred to the larger and more formal apartments of the household. My Aunt Diane entered with a flourish when she was announced.

I saw that she was dressed in an elaborate way, and her huge hat with its spray of plumes told me that the visit was a formal one, and had importance in her eyes. In spite of the pain which the sight of her brought to me, I begged her to be seated, and proffered an infusion of tea. Both civilities were rejected by my aunt with a wave of her kid gloved hand. She fixed me with an unwinking gaze, and began to speak to me without more ado.

'I have come to ask you to retire from

Anthony's life,' she said.

I rose to my feet at these words; shaken in spite of my attempts to armour myself against the disquiet her presence brought me, and the trials which I guessed were to come. 'I am at a loss to understand your words,' I replied. 'I think you should explain yourself, or retract so unseemly and incomprehensible a remark.'

'Do not play the innocent with me,' Diane said. 'I know your sort. Innocent on the surface and full of guile beneath. Do you want the matter spelled out to you? It should be clear to you, without words. I am asking you to withdraw from Anthony Lycett's life, so that I can take my rightful place by his side.'

'You speak of a rightful place,' I countered. 'Yet I believe there is no legal tie between my husband and yourself. What happened in the past was an affaire only, which I believe now to be over.'

'Then you do not believe the truth,' Diane answered. 'This matter between Anthony and myself is not over. And indeed, is scarcely begun.'

Diane eyed me calculatingly, then resumed, 'You must know that I love Anthony totally, and I loved him for years, before ever you came on the scene.'

'I know that mine was a marriage of convenience,' I replied. 'But what led up to the marriage of convenience is finished. You cannot recreate the past in the present, when immediate circumstances have changed.'

'So, we have a philosopher in the family,' jeered Diane. 'A sophist. A Jesuit, next. Let me tell you that my relationship with Anthony was more intense and closer than your own. Do you know that I conceived his child?'

'Why no,' I was greatly taken aback by this statement, and indeed such a circumstance had not entered into my reckoning. 'I thought that would make you pause,' Diane said. 'I conceived Anthony's child two years ago, to my great joy. But unfortunately I had a fall, and the baby miscarried.'

'But how can you be sure that this child was my husband's?' I cried. 'You were a married woman then. Surely the child belonged to Sir Toby, by rights?'

'Toby was totally incapable in every sense,' Diane said, and the callousness of her tone affected me deeply. 'Toby did not know of the child, of course. No-one knew. Not even that busybody Bloomingfield. I went to Bath to take the cure, and all traces of the event were eliminated, during my treatment at that spa.'

Again the coldness of the tone shocked me. 'But why has Anthony never mentioned this matter to me?' I asked my aunt. 'Why has he kept secret a matter which so vitally concerned you both?'

'No doubt he did not wish to damage himself in your eyes,' Diane said. 'And men are notoriously squeamish about mentioning these affairs.'

'So there is only your unsubstantiated word in this matter,' I replied. 'It is your word alone which apportions blame and makes you bring this painful story to me now.'

'But *you* have not given Anthony a child,' Diane said accusingly. 'You have given him no family, although there has been time.'

'The relations of my husband and myself are private,' I told Diane. 'And their outcome is private also, to the whole world. And not least to yourself.'

'Do not come the high and mighty with me, my girl. It is through my offices that you are where you find yourself now,' countered Diane.

'It is I who brought you from the obscurity of the country to London, and into Anthony Lycett's life. You have everything to thank me for. Do not forget it. I will stand no insolence from you.'

'You are forgetting yourself surely, to speak to me thus,' I replied. A dreadful searing rage possessed me as I spoke. I faced my aunt with opposition and fire. I felt my colour heighten, and knew that anger flashed in my eyes. She halted her discourse and considered me calmly.

'You speak of private relationships between husband and wife,' she said. 'But you have nothing to boast about. Rather the reverse.

'Your marriage was not consummated upon your wedding night, was it? Your husband was absent from your house, and absent from your presence, and absent from your bed.

'Why, Felicity? Have you asked yourself why?

'Because he was with me. Anthony spent your wedding night with me, in our private rear-room at Rivermead House.

'We slept as usual upon our private bed. We made love. We kissed and pleased one another. He slept at last in my arms, and not in yours. That is where your husband, Anthony, was. He spent the night hours of your wedding-day, with me.'

* * *

It was at this moment that Mrs Colgate knocked at the door of the room, and entered with a tray bearing an infusion of tea, and some sweetmeats.

She glanced from one to another, as we stood facing each other. The atmosphere of the room must have been like that before a storm-cloud breaks; or a hurricane blows itself out. She murmured some civilities, and then withdrew.

I poured the tea, but neither of us could eat or drink. I felt distracted by the encounter, and Diane appeared distraught and in some duality of mind. 'Think everything over,' she said. 'Consider what I have told you, and I will be in touch with you again.' She then left me without another word.

That night, Anthony came to me as I lay alone in bed in my room. I saw him enter the bedchamber in the shaded light of the lamp, and remarked his night-robe of silk with the fine linen shift, beneath.

He sat for a moment on the bed, and regarded me. But at his presence in this intimate moment, it was as if my body turned to stone; and my mind was frozen into a clamp of opposition and rejection.

I knew that tears ran from my eyes, and down my face, and began to soak the pillow. Anthony regarded me intently, and then drew me towards him in a passionate embrace.

I found that I was quite unable to accept his advances towards the accustomed marital intimacy; not the ideal of female submission to the dominant male, so prevalent at this time, could unfreeze the icy cast in which I lay.

He entered the bed, and attempted with his skilled and tender caresses, to free my body and mind from their shackles. But without result. I found I could not accept him in conjugal intimacy. That such an idea was abhorrent to me. I lay beside him like a figure on a sarcophagus, carved in stone.

Anthony dried my eyes of their tears and began to question me. He was greatly taken aback by my attitude, for I had been a willing partner previously, and had found pleasure in his commitment. But I could not reply to his questions. It was as if words themselves had also been frozen within me. Indeed, life itself seemed to be in suspension; this is how it must be, I thought, before one passes away.

At last Anthony desisted from his physical attempts to arouse me, and sank back upon the pillows of the bed. I saw his handsome face grave and disturbed in the lamplight, and the fine embroidery on the collar of his nightshift. He lay for a moment, without saying a word.

Then he roused himself from the bed. 'I have never forced a woman to accept me, in all my life,' Anthony Lycett said. 'Not a paid harlot, and not a woman of the court. And I will not so force my own wife.'

Anthony then got up from the bed, drew on his silken night-robe. I watched his tall figure cross the room; softly he closed the door, and he was gone.

*   *   *

It was inevitable that within a few days we should discuss this matter, which was of such great importance to us both. Anthony and I sat alone in the salon. Paul and Louisa were in the study employing themselves playing on the harpsichord and singing tender ballads. Between the two, it seemed, a further closeness and amity had been reached.

'It is clear to me that you have learned some of the history of the past,' Anthony began. We were taking a little wine. It was after the evening meal. Apart from the faint tinkle of the harpsichord the big house was still. 'But I beg you to allow me to make some explanations.

'I am told that Diane called to see you, privately, only recently. I can well guess the stories she told you, and the effect these would have upon you.'

I did not reply to this, not wishing to make a serious matter more grave by accusations and reproaches. I waited for him to go on.

'It is true that Diane introduced you to me as a prospective wife, and that later we married so that I could fulfil the conditions of my late uncle's trust, and so inherit his fortune and estate.

'I was grateful to you. I liked you. But I did not love you. You were unknown to me, and though acceptable as a means to the desired end, yet I saw our alliance as no more than a legal tie I must endure. And then, for me, everything changed.

'For after our wedding, when we began to live in the same house, and enjoy our proximity, and share our joint interests, I began to see you in a new light. Pleasure in your company and satisfaction in our companionship turned to deep affection. Within a very short time, Felicity, love was born within me, and this love has now grown and flowered, so that...

'I adore you now, deeply and intensely, and with a strong, constant and burning ardour. I have never loved any woman as I love you, my dear wife. No-one has ever engaged my affections, my hopes and my allegiance as have you. You are the lodestar of my life. And I ask for no other companion for the rest of my days.'

I was greatly affected by this speech of Anthony's which I knew to be sincere and spoken from his deepest heart. He was not a man to reveal his private feelings easily, I well knew. And to find that he could tell me of his emotions so frankly and coherently made a deep impression upon my mind. I waited for him to go on.

'I would like to defend myself against the charges laid upon me by Diane,' Anthony told me. 'Will you tell me what these were, so that I can justify myself?'

'Diane's accusations were not so much against yourself, as against me,' I answered gravely. I remembered the scorn she had poured upon me, because I had not so far borne Anthony a child.

I wondered if I should mention her statement that she had conceived Anthony's child; but as I was unsure as to the truth of this, I decided to keep silence upon this circumstance. Again, I did not wish to add fuel to a fire already bright.

'If she informed you that she had conceived my child,' Anthony interposed, 'I had already heard this on the gossip circle of the court. But the child was not mine. For I was on active service in France for the Duke at all material times. The child was another's. But who this was, has never been revealed.'

I accepted this explanation from Anthony, and believed what he said. I added, 'But the matter of our wedding night caused me great pain. For you were absent when I was prepared for you, and longed to receive you into my bed, and give you myself.

'Do not forget that I loved you deeply and fervently, at this time,' I told Anthony. 'You must have seen my love. The love of an unschooled and ardent girl, overcome by her first experience of adoration and longing.

'To flout this love was a serious matter, and one calculated to undermine our relationship, and our future life together.'

'I accept your reproaches, and indeed, your rebukes to me are not more severe than my reproaches to myself,' Anthony answered me.

'But Diane insisted that I should spend my wedding night with her. We had been lovers for some time, it was true, and she was suddenly afraid that my marriage might mitigate against the continuation of our relationship.

'She decided to exercise her authority over me, and her opposition to yourself. She insisted that I should spend that night with her, as her lover, or ... She would inform the trustees of my uncle's will of our collusion, and that my marriage to you was a façade only, undergone only to procure my inheritance.

'You must understand the power of these trustees, Felicity. It was within their power, at that exact moment, to withhold my inheritance, even though the papers had been signed. For by the Deed of Covenant, they had to satisfy themselves as to the validity of my marriage.

'It was within their power, at that time, to withhold the money I had sought so ardently. If they thought there had been a plot, a cynical manipulation in order to deceive them, they could have reacted instantly. And the actual transference of the estate would have been delayed for enquiries—or halted altogether.

'All would have been in vain, our marriage, and the wedding arrangements. I had to comply with Diane's request. I had no alternative. But I assure you ... Felicity ... I assure you ...

'I have never since that time approached Diane, or have been intimate with her. Soon after that night the trustees were satisfied as to my good faith, the will became valid, and the estate was handed over to me. Diane could not force me to her will again. And since that time ...

'I assure you of my love, its growth and its culmination in passion and commitment. Believe me, I beg of you, Felicity. I have truly revealed the truth, and all that is in my heart.'

Anthony left his chair and knelt before me

upon one knee, and took my hands into his own. He covered my hands with kisses and raised his face so that his eyes could gaze into mine.

I believed him. I accepted all that he had said. The explanations were full and explicit, and fitted entirely the previous doubts and painful circumstances. Yet I felt no sense of relief or lightening of the heavy places within my own heart.

It was as if the preceding shafts of pain had hurt me beyond recovery of their injuries. The revelation of the plot; the distress of hearing of the miscarried child—although discounted, yet its wounds remained. The humiliation of my wedding night, my earlier love which had been discounted and ignored ... It seemed that all these facts had left an area of anguish within me, nothing—not even Anthony's protestations of the truth—could remove or assuage.

Anthony rose and sat beside me on the velvet settle, still holding my hands, and gazing into my face. We sat so without saying a word for sometime; until the silence from the study told us that the harpsichord was no longer being played, and that shortly Paul and Louisa would return.

When they came into the room, Anthony and I were sitting apart, not conversing, as married couples often do. But neither Paul nor Louisa could have known of the regret which filled us. Of the anguish which was in both our hearts.

CHAPTER TWELVE

Within a few days a circumstance concerning Louisa began to cause me great concern. She began to show all the signs of mental instability; and indeed, her condition was both unseemly and alarming.

Again she roamed about the house, crying and in great distress. She yearned for Charles Latham, she said. She tried repeatedly to get out of the house, and once she threw a chamber utensil out of a closed window. The maids began to dread to serve her, and Mrs Colgate complained. I was at my wits' end as to what to do.

Towards the conclusion of our discourse together, Anthony had said to me earnestly:

'I beg you to stay in my life, Felicity. I could not bear it if you should now decide to depart.

'Even if you feel you cannot love me...' for Anthony had been sensible of my feelings and reactions, although these had not been put into words, '... I implore you to remain at Beaufroy House. I could not face the future without you, here in my home, and by my side.

'I will do everything to woo you afresh, and perhaps in time, you may discover your earlier feelings for me. Do not despair. I will make every effort to recreate your love. I ask you only to remain at Beaufroy House, and that we may continue, outwardly, as man and wife. In time, I am certain, I can recreate our happiness, again.'

And so I had agreed to remain. And indeed, in a strange way I had come to love Beaufroy House, and I rejoiced that the interior was now so greatly improved; and that happiness reigned among the staff, and visitors to our domain.

But I knew that, without Anthony's earnest appeal, I would have quit this home; though where I would have gone I did not know, and could not bring myself to envisage.

Again I appealed to Paul for help concerning Louisa, but his reply was not encouraging. 'Louisa lacks both discipline and self-control,' Paul said. 'I cannot get her to see reason, concerning her residence here, and her stay in England. And believe me, at this moment, I have more serious matters on my mind.'

He tempered his uncompromising reply with his usual frank and open smile. He said no more, and yet I was left with an impression of both sympathy and understanding. Indeed, he later brought me a small nosegay of flowers, and as he placed this in my hands he said, 'So many things pass, Felicity. All of life, and our efforts too.'

The words were enigmatic, and I could not

understand them. But I knew in that moment that Paul had realized, with a deep intuition, much that was private between myself and Anthony. He seemed to stand like a rock for me in the shifting sands, in the ebb and flow of circumstance and reaction. And I was deeply grateful to him.

And yet, in spite of Paul's realistic approach to Louisa's problems, I fancied that he was drawn towards her.

Often I caught him looking at her indulgently; and she in her turn played up to his attentions, and was more than willing to be the focus of his goodwill.

Indeed, I sometimes thought that they were more than usually attracted to one another. I could not understand how this realization caused me such pain. It was as if their growing closeness seemed to emphasize my own solitary state; and their deepening friendliness seemed to throw into relief my love for my husband which had been so ardent, and which had now entirely died. Indeed, Anthony himself noticed the change in Paul's general attitude.

'I think that Paul is in love,' Anthony told me. 'I know all the signs, and can discern them in him! Yet I do not know who the lady can be,' Anthony added.

'It is perhaps a young person at the Prince Regent's court, for Paul has been venturing out recently to social gatherings which he did not frequent, before.'

'Do you think the lady whom he prefers could be—Louisa?' I ventured.

Anthony was astounded. 'How could that be possible?' he asked me.

'Louisa is betrothed to Charles Latham, and I believe honours her attachment to him greatly. No. You are mistaken, Felicity. You have misjudged his kindliness and consideration towards Louisa for something deeper.

'And do not forget that, in a way, Louisa is Paul's guest and he is responsible for her. And they travelled through Europe together, on their way to Beaufroy House, so that the bonds of their friendship must have been closely forged. But as for anything else...' Anthony laughed at me in kindly fashion, and raised his glass towards me in a salute. 'Come drink your wine and forget such a wild speculation.'

Yet I could not forget my conclusions, and indeed, the possibility of their attachment seemed to haunt me. Yet why should it? Why should I be appalled? Those in engagements changed their minds frequently, I told myself. An engagement was not so binding as marriage, after all. Paul and Louisa were at liberty to forge their own lives. I only knew that the prospect of their love was like a further wound in my heart.

A few days after this conversation, I was about to descend the stairs into the main hall of

Beaufroy House, when I saw Paul and Anthony standing together close to the foot of the stairs. Their voices carried to me quite plainly.

'... but why should you ask such a question of me?' Paul was saying. 'This is the most private of matters, and can be only vouchsafed when all doubts are over, and the final conclusion is arranged.'

'I ask you out of interest, Paul,' Anthony responded to his cousin. 'Your well-being is a matter of great concern to me, and I would not wish any harm to befall you in this new area of your life.

'You have had no romantic attachment until now. And indeed, your whole life has been spent in country pursuits and in the service of the Duke.

'You have not frequented balls, soirées, gaming clubs, and the like. And your name has never been linked with a young lady's, until now.'

'And my name is not linked romantically with anyone at the present time,' Paul answered rather vehemently, I thought. He seemed not pleased by Anthony's questioning. And indeed, would have quitted the hall had not Anthony put out his hand, and detained the younger man before him.

'I reserve the right to conduct my own affairs,' Paul continued. 'My preference is no concern of yours.'

'So you have a preference,' Anthony pressed. 'You greatly like, or have fallen in love with some young lady, and this affects you deeply.

'Come now. Own up. I will not betray your confidence. But to be aware of the intimate feelings of a close member of the family prevents hurt, and often eases the way forward.

'Thus regard my interest, Paul. I assure you it is nothing more.'

Paul hesitated, and then said rather grudgingly I thought, 'It is true I care deeply for a lady of my acquaintance. But she is not aware of my attachment, and indeed would not welcome the knowledge in the least.'

'So, she is given to another,' Anthony said. 'Is this in marriage, in engagement, or in understanding?'

'I am not at liberty to say any more,' Paul answered. 'And indeed, in putting my feelings into words I have done myself no service, since the sentiments I bear for this lady must be kept totally hidden, lest they cause extensive harm.'

'I understand.' Anthony laid his arm around Paul's shoulders, as if regretting that he had pressed the younger man so far. 'Come, let us go over the French maps together. To pursue our work will take our minds off the more tender emotions which clearly cause you perplexity and pain.'

Paul smiled at Anthony, clearly understanding and appreciating Anthony's interest in his welfare. Together they moved, side by side, down the hall towards the formal study, where I knew their maps and the accoutrements of their trade were stored.

I stood quite still at the head of the stairs. Although I knew that my action in remaining just out of sight of the two men and listening to their private conversation, was unorthodox, and perhaps open to blame; yet I could not censure myself, for I felt that, in those few minutes, I had gained information of importance to my whole life.

There was no doubt but that Paul was falling in love. And with Louisa. The lady in question must be Louisa, for she was bound in an engagement to Charles Latham, which made her forbidden to Paul, as a man of honour, and as her joint legal custodian in this country.

And what of Louisa's feelings for Paul? I did not know. I dreaded to find out. Distress again engulfed my beleaguered and aching heart.

And now, my Aunt Rebecca came to stay with us at Beaufroy House. This visit was overdue, and had been delayed by an illness, not serious, which had prevented her from travelling. I was more than overjoyed to see my relation, and drew her swiftly into the house and the salon. We sat by the fire and took refreshment. Our voices rang through the room as we recounted our news, and brought one another up to date with family matters.

I was struck by the fact that my aunt looked

frailer than before. Her mind was as vigorous as ever, and her tongue more trenchant, if that was possible. But she leaned a little on the furniture when she moved; and was glad to remain seated. I could not help but feel concern on her behalf.

It was not long before she had sized up the circumstances in Beaufroy House. 'You are desperately unhappy. What has gone wrong? To what situation have you come, Felicity?' she asked me.

'I thought your marriage must be harmonious and straightforward, for you wrote to me upon your betrothal that you were deeply in love, and longed only to be the wife of the man who had proposed to you.

'Yet now, clearly your passion has waned, while his has grown. And this other woman in the house. She is a troublemaker, and will lead to no good.

'There are undercurrents here. People are pulling different ways. There is no harmony; no solution. I do not like the situation in which you find yourself, at all.'

In vain I tried to soothe her, and reassure her that there was nothing amiss between Anthony and myself; for I did not wish her to be concerned.

'You have grown beautiful,' she added. 'You were always attractive, at Pomfret Magna, though you did not always believe this. But now you have gained confidence, and your good looks have blossomed. Your dresses become you, and you move with grace. There is no doubt that Lord Anthony must be gratified to have you by his side.'

I murmured some refutation, though I was glad to have her praise, which was without self-seeking, and sincere. Aunt Rebecca instantly liked both Paul and Anthony; but Louisa she could not abear, and she often appeared deaf when Louisa was in our company.

It was inevitable, of course, that Aunt Rebecca should journey to Rivermead House to call upon my other aunt, Diane Bullough. She set off in the carriage alone, as I was occupied at home at the time of the appointment. Upon her return I could see that she had serious news to impart.

'Diane tells me a strange tale about this French countess being entertained in your home,' she began. 'Diane informs me that this woman's residence here is known throughout court circles, and there is grave consternation and considerable gossip about this situation.

'I do not need to tell you that we are at war with France. That French nationals are barred from this country, and all things French are frowned upon. But of course you know this. You are not stupid, Felicity. You knew this at Pomfret Magna. Even perfumes are not now imported and French fashions rejected with scorn.

'Yet to be entertaining this so-called French aristocrat here gives the impression that the Lycett family are siding with the French. That their sympathies are with our enemies. That there are traitors at Beaufroy House who are not true to their own side. Needless to say, such an imputation is serious indeed.'

'Aunt Rebecca!' I cried. 'How can you take such futile gossip seriously? Louisa is being entertained here at the direct request of the military command. I assure you there is no complicity. No treason. How can you heed Diane's words when you know in your heart they are not true?'

'I may know,' answered my Aunt Rebecca. 'Yet do others also know the truth?

'I am told you made enemies at court, when you stole Lord Anthony Lycett from under the noses of other, more experienced ladies, who had placed themselves at his disposal for marriage—or any other course.

'The Prince Regent is displeased with you for some reason. It appears that your marrying Anthony baulked him of a large sum of money, though I do not know how.

'Your instant success at court displeased many who had tried in vain to reach the inner circles. Your success made you enemies, Felicity. And now they are prepared to strike.'

'To strike, Aunt Rebecca? Why whatever do you mean?'

'Listen Felicity, and I will tell you. Your

Aunt Diane is particularly incensed against you concerning this charge of treason. For her late husband, Sir Toby, was a dedicated government servant, she informed me, and they were both committed wholeheartedly to the British cause.

'So strongly does Diane feel about this that she has ... She has visited Lord Castlereagh, the Prime Minister, and has denounced you. She accuses you of being a traitor to your country and the king.

'It appears that there is a leakage of information upon military matters, which is well known to the inner circles of the court,' my aunt continued. 'It is suggested that the French woman guest at Beaufroy House is not one lady, but a succession of ladies of French nationality, who act as couriers, taking abroad secret information to the French high command. It is rumoured that ...'

'Are both you and Diane out of your minds?' I cried in consternation. I rose to my feet, quite astounded by this recital of bogus and falsified information. 'It is not possible to refute these charges in detail, but I assure you Aunt Rebecca, there is no truth in them. And these accusations are lies and without foundation upon fact.'

'So you may believe, Felicity, and so I myself may believe too. But will the outside world believe this, at the present time?

'Indeed, Diane put her case against you

persuasively. She assured me that Lord Anthony and Paul Lycett were not so much blamed as yourself. You are the scapegoat and the offender. It is against yourself that Diane lays the charges. I urge you most strongly to assemble the truth of the matter, and to prepare your own defence.'

Aunt Rebecca was quite overcome at this point, and had to be assisted to her room by Mrs Colgate. I sat alone in the salon pondering the situation. It was not long before the truth of the matter came to my mind.

So this was Diane's way of wreaking vengeance upon both Anthony and myself; but principally upon myself. I remembered her threats of retaliation. And I knew that her method of revenge was severe and subtle indeed.

For that a serving soldier's wife should be charged with transmitting information to the enemy, would be damaging indeed to his name and career. And Paul too, must surely lose credence in the eyes of those he served and who had always trusted him.

That the charges were false and bogus, who was to know? For the essence of espionage work is that it is secret, undercover, hidden, known to only the chosen few. And nothing of the inner complexities could be revealed by ourselves at Beaufroy House. We had but few weapons with which to defend ourselves. And particularly to defend myself.

I paced the room in some perplexity of mind concerning these events. But before I could decide on any future course, other developments overtook me. My husband, Anthony, returned home.

He told me without ado that he had been summoned to meet Lord Castlereagh in his cabinet room, and that there, these charges concerning myself had been laid frankly before him.

Of course Anthony refuted the accusations strongly. He told me Lord Castlereagh listened carefully, and gave him his attention. But one circumstance emerged from this interview which astounded Anthony, and caused him great concern.

He found, and indeed it was quite obvious, that there was no liaison between the government of the country and the military forces.

Lord Castlereagh did not know, in detail, what the Duke of Wellington was doing. He was not aware of the loss of Charles Latham, and the danger this represented to the success of the Duke's military operations. Lord Castlereagh sought information. But in return, he had none to give.

It was at this point that Anthony requested the attention of his military chief, and the Duke of Wellington had personally intervened. The Duke had privately received both Lord Castlereagh and Anthony at Apsley

House, and had given the Prime Minister an abridged and guarded account of the espionage matters in hand.

Lord Castlereagh was quite satisfied, so Anthony informed me, that the rumours and accusations concerning myself were false. But, he added, he had no way of stopping the gossip currently running through social circles in London, and which might certainly cause Anthony, myself and our household, inconvenience and pain.

The Duke of Wellington had withdrawn from the situation. He was well known for his impatience with politicians, and the political mode of life. He had ordered Anthony to continue his work among the agents. Nothing was changed. Both Anthony and Paul were to proceed.

But Lord Castlereagh made a strong suggestion that I myself should leave London for a time, in order to allow the scandal to die down.

As Anthony had, in a way, scored a victory over the Prime Minister by the intervention of the Duke of Wellington, he had agreed to put to me this course.

'I urge you to accept it, Felicity,' Anthony told me. 'I have an estate in the country, called Guissley Manor, which is secluded and private, and set amid the charming woodlands of Berkshire. I will order them to prepare the house for you, and you can take a holiday there.

'Paul and I will visit you frequently. You will not be alone. But we must honour this request, my dear. The Duke has ordered me to humour the Prime Minister. And it is our duty that you should quit London, and that we should obey this directive from the high command.'

So saying, Anthony poured a glass of wine for me, as we sat together after his belated evening meal. But I sat with the wine before me, and could not drink. I did not know it, but tears had come, unbidden, into my eyes.

CHAPTER THIRTEEN

Immediately after these foregoing events, Anthony had of course gone round post haste to Rivermead House, to interview Diane.

He was bent upon asking her for an explanation of her conduct, and of impressing upon her the harm to us all her actions had wrought; and to urge her to do all that she could to put matters right.

But he found the house empty and closed; an aged gardener told him that Lady Diane had gone to Wells, for the cure; and no-one knew when she would be expected back.

Anthony then called at the duty room of the Duke's London headquarters. He found there grave news concerning the military matters in hand.

Upon his return to Beaufroy House, Anthony called us all into the drawing-room. We sat down in silence and waited for him to speak.

Yet I felt abstracted, and had to will myself to attend to Anthony's words. For I had been packing my clothes in my valise, prior to being taken to Guissley Manor. I felt dejected and put down. I had been blamed for a fault that was not mine, I thought, and which concerned a military situation beyond my control.

Yet even so, Anthony's words penetrated my abstraction. I began to listen carefully to what he had to say.

'A serious situation has arisen concerning the second agent, William Lansbury, who was instructed, while already in France, to attempt to locate Charles Latham and to escort him home,' Anthony began.

'You will know that David Exeter, the first agent despatched into France, was quite unable to trace the hiding-place of Charles, and was forced to abandon his mission and return to this country.

'And now, the second agent, William Lansbury, has been apprehended by the French forces and thrown into prison.'

'What has been his fate?' asked Paul, and I saw the skin around his mouth tighten, and his colour paled a little. He clearly knew what to expect.

'Lansbury was tortured and then killed. His body was flung on a dung heap, and there it was found, decomposed, by a courier who was Lansbury's friend. William had been mutilated before he died.

'He of course carried no despatches, and he was a cool officer, who carried a vast amount of military information in his memory. But how much he was forced to reveal before he died, we do not know.'

There was a pause. And then I said, 'I think you are trying to tell us, Anthony, that it is now imperative that Charles Latham be reached and brought out of France without more ado.'

'Precisely.' He turned to Louisa. 'In spite of all your information and instructions, the hiding-place of Charles remains undiscovered. It seems to me that there is only one person who can lead us to where Charles is in safe keeping. And that is yourself.'

'With that I agree,' said Louisa, and suddenly she assumed a dignity and a purpose I had not observed in her before. 'I know where he is, and I can lead you there.'

'Concerning myself,' said Anthony, 'I have been ordered to remain in London at the Duke's military headquarters. Paul has been selected for this mission, as we expected. And you are ordered to depart, Paul, without delay.'

'I am more than ready,' Paul said, rising to his feet. 'Has cover been arranged for Louisa and myself? We travelled as mendicants when we quit France. But I doubt that such a disguise would serve us again.'

'The matter of your disguises has already been discussed at headquarters,' Anthony replied. 'And the head of security has suggested to me that this mission could well be attempted by three people, instead of two.

'He is of the opinion that a small group of people travelling together, with a legitimate excuse and authentic papers, must be less noticeable than a young man and a woman travelling together, unescorted and alone.'

'I think he is right,' Anthony finished. 'He is therefore attempting to find the third man to accompany Paul, and you, Louisa.'

There was silence in the room. 'Or this third person could be a woman,' I heard myself say. 'This would be more natural still. A small family party say, travelling to a funeral or other family gathering.

'An aunt and a niece,' I said. 'Or two sisters, with Paul the brother.' I turned to Anthony. 'I see no reason,' I said, 'why I myself cannot accompany Paul and Louisa abroad. There is no reason why I cannot aid and assist them, and give them the disguise and support they need.

'Indeed, don't you see,' I cried, 'that this is the ideal solution for several of our problems?

'I cannot bear to be sent to the manor house in Berkshire. I cannot bear to be incarcerated there, alone. But for me to travel to France with Paul and Louisa, upon this mission which must be executed... Surely that would answer all our questions? Surely that would fulfil all the conditions I myself, and the military command, and the Prime Minister would require?

'I should be out of London society. Indeed, out of the country for a time. The Prime Minister has exonerated me from all blame concerning the charges Diane levelled against me, so that surely I shall be acceptable to the security command?

'And indeed, the security forces have no charge against me, but have known full well that I and everyone in this household have been merely obeying the Duke of Wellington's orders in entertaining Louisa here.

'So that... Allow me to go, I beg of you.' I turned to Paul. 'Paul, say you will permit me to help you. I assure you I would give the mission my most devoted services. Anthony, give me your blessing. Louisa, say you will accept me. I beg of you all to allow me to go.'

*   *   *

There was complete silence in the room at these words, and I saw a glance of consternation and dismay pass between the two men. And then Louisa was speaking.

'I think this is a feasible idea. I hated the last

journey across France, with only Paul to guide and attend me. Oh, do not misunderstand me, Paul. Your presence was entirely agreeable to me, and your kindness and care for me outstanding.

'Yet I missed the company of another woman. A maid. I was obligated to wash out my own hose each evening, and to carry my own possessions in a bag! So that, to have another woman on the journey with me would be ideal. For Felicity could travel with me as my servant. Felicity could be my attendant and my maid.'

The coolness of this suggestion took my breath away. Yet Louisa saw nothing incongruous in this proposal. 'Felicity has had training in the more mundane matters of life, I am told,' she was continuing. 'For she lived in humble circumstances before her marriage, and is used to the rougher aspect of life.'

Before I could speak, Paul took up the cudgels on my behalf. 'Your statement is not strictly true, Louisa,' he told her. 'Felicity was not of the royal court before her marriage, but she comes from an old and respected family in Somerset, and her education and upbringing have been admirable.'

'I meant no offence, of course,' answered Louisa. 'But I am of an ancient French aristocratic family, and my provenance is well known. I mention this only to stress the suitability of Felicity being my maid. I shall enjoy to travel through France properly caparisoned, and with my own servant at my beck and call.'

I motioned to Paul not to pursue the matter further. Louisa's intransigence hurt me no longer; and I guessed that at this moment she was overcome with joy at the thought of returning to France and seeing her fiancé, Charles Latham, again.

It was now, after this exchange between Louisa and myself that Anthony tried to dissuade me from my course. To my surprise Paul joined his persuasions to my husband's, and together the two men put forward reasons, explanations, and jointly reinforced their arguments to me to stay at home.

But my mind was quite made up. If the unknown chief of security at headquarters agreed, I would throw in my lot with the two travellers, and venture into France. I awaited then the news from the barracks that my offer had been accepted. I waited to know the next step in the surprising course of my life.

Later I was to wonder at the vehemence of my wish to quit Beaufroy House, and to depart upon this errand into the unknown.

I faced the fact now, squarely, that lately life at Beaufroy House had wearied me. In a strange way, now that the decorations and re-arrangements of the house were complete, it sometimes seemed that I had nothing further to do there, and my time of usefulness in the huge mansion was over.

And also, the failure of my love for Anthony had cast a shadow over my life at Beaufroy House. Had our love survived and endured; had our love for one another grown and blossomed; had our joint existence been fruitful and heart-warming—then I would not have desired, so ardently to have quit my home and present life. Invisible strings would have held me. The atmosphere of love would have kept me at least within the sphere of Anthony's influence and regard.

But now that I had taken this step, it was as if the adventure itself called to me. As if the change in my circumstances I now so ardently sought would not be denied. I saw Anthony's distraught face before me; the pleading in his shadowed eyes. But I knew I would not respond to his entreaties to remain. I knew that this was the moment I must obey the secret prompting of my nature. I knew that if at all possible, I must go.

'But this is not a permanent parting, Anthony,' I told my husband. 'I shall return. We will take up our life again.' I will not leave you, I thought. You have begged me to stay within your life. And I will honour and accede to your request.

Very shortly, the formal permission I awaited was received from the military headquarters. Full and frank investigations had been made, and the security authorities were satisfied upon all points. The Marchioness of Glenivray would be permitted to travel with Lieutenant Paul Lycett and the Countess de Courcy, into France, upon the errand privately specified.

The disguise would be that of a married woman travelling from Calais to Paris, to visit her sick mother. Her male cousin would be with her. And she would be accompanied by her maid.

But the further instructions amazed and astounded me. For the Marchioness of Glenivray will be journeying as the middle-class wife of a tradesman. And the Countess de Courcy would accompany her in an inferior position. The countess would be her attendant, and her personal maid.

* * *

There were shrieks of protest and cries of refutation. Again I saw all the signs of mental derangement in Louisa's behaviour and protest. But Anthony quelled this outburst at once.

'Louisa, if you desire to return to France and your fiancé, Charles Latham again, you must make this journey escorted by Paul, and now Felicity in the guise specified.

'I ask you, nay, I order you to accept the disciplines of this course. Not to do so will endanger your own life, and the lives of those who will accompany you.'

When we were alone, Anthony said, 'How can I part with you upon this undertaking? I would rather face a thousand deaths at the hands of the French forces, than that you should run into the slightest danger.'

I felt touched by his grief and concern, which I knew were genuine, and came from the heart. Yet I felt unable to comfort him by my proximity and the granting of intimacy. He seemed to accept this withdrawal on my part; and yet, this marital aloofness clearly added to his sorrow.

Events now moved apace. Within a short time clothes arrived for the three of us, fashioned to fit the characters in France, we must assume.

For myself there was a well-made and sober dress and cloak of dark grey worsted material. It was now early in the year of 1815, and the weather was cold; snow and ice were threatened. With this dress was an outfit of thick woollen underwear, no doubt the quality and style befitting a lady of provincial position and worth. A blue bonnet topped this ensemble, which came well down upon my head, and hid a great part of my hair and my face.

I saw that Paul's suit was that of a qualified artisan. Clearly, I myself had married into a higher branch of trade, and had left my humble beginning behind. Louisa was proffered a coat and dress of stout and already well-worn black woollen-mixture. Her bonnet was large and unbecoming. And upon her feet there were to be sabot-type boots covering vast and stoutly ribbed hose. She had garters to match of plain cotton. She was ordered never to wear gauntlets upon her hands.

Louisa accepted her new wardrobe in sulky silence. She spoke to no-one; she did not even appear pleased now to be leaving London, and returning to her native land. Even the prospect of seeing Charles again, failed to lighten her spirits. She continued aloof, cold, and as always, unappreciative of all that was done.

Colonel Forsyth, the head of security, came to see us. He was a tall, agile man, a colonel in the Dragoons, clearly a firm disciplinarian with an astute and far-seeing attitude of mind. He questioned Louisa and myself and gave us a brief lecture. He finally asked us to take the oath of allegiance.

'You are both now on active service,' he told us, when this had been done. 'I have never sworn in women previously. I hope my judgement on this occasion is not at fault.

'I am now your commanding officer, stationed at the Duke of Wellington's headquarters in London. My second-in-command is Captain the Marquis of Glenivray, your husband, ma'am,' the colonel added to myself.

'But your officer in the field will be

Lieutenant Paul Lycett. You must obey him implicitly. You must trust his judgement at all times, and his assessment of any situation. On a mission of this nature there is no room for individual action, for personal evaluation. You must trust Lieutenant Lycett with your lives. He will not let you be put down.

'Lieutenant Lycett is a skilled officer, who has been trained by myself. He knows France well, and all aspects of French life. And his knowledge of French military matters is second to none.'

When we were alone Louisa began to weep again; and I gathered that this time she regretted leaving London and Beaufroy House. It was very difficult to understand and be patient with this wilful and contradictory girl.

Indeed, Colonel Forsyth told Anthony, 'I do not envy your wife travelling with the countess. She is a difficult customer, that one. If she were not essential to the operation I would never agree to her journeying to France. But she and she alone knows where Charles Latham is hidden, and can lead us to him. She is a vital and necessary adjunct to this cause. But God help those who must accompany her, and with whom she must spend her days.'

And upon this sombre note from the head of the Duke of Wellington's espionage service in London, we prepared to depart.

We could not see what lay ahead, or what

had to be undergone. Or of the vast changes in all our circumstances our errand into France would bring.

We could not be aware of the gathering military storms which would rend Europe in two; and reforge continental history. We did not know that the events of our journey would change us; and change all our lives.

CHAPTER FOURTEEN

We travelled in Anthony's private carriage to Dover, where we embarked upon a maintenance ship travelling to France. The ship was low in the water with provisions and equipment, and we were rather coldly received by the captain, who was obeying orders with ill grace.

He clearly thought that three extra human passengers were displacing a great deal of military cargo necessary to our armies overseas. Paul answered him in a civil and conciliatory way, and the atmosphere eased.

Our quarters were spartan; amenities were at a minimum. I was suddenly glad of my thick dress and cloak and long undergarments of wool. But Louisa could not bear this untreated wool upon her skin. And she constantly scratched herself in a realistic and rather uncouth way.

I pondered Paul's earlier instructions to us. 'When you assume an identity, you must not do this by the adoption of some surface characteristics, but by the acceptance of the true nature of the part you have to play.

'In short, you must *become* the person you wish to be. You must not, except in the deepest privacy, utter words which belong to your past, and your real nature. Speak only in French, and as from your new identities. Forget the past, and leave your English personalities behind.'

He set us a fine example by his portrayal of the French artisan he was supposed to be. Within his pouch were bills paid and unpaid, which showed that he was beginning a small business as a wheelwright in Calais. He carried the tools of his trade, which was usual at this time. For these were valuable items to a man who worked with his hands.

Within my own reticule and pockets were letters which revealed me as Madame Eloise Mairan, also of Calais. I had family letters upon my person, including one from my mother's housekeeper in Paris, telling me that my parent was seriously ill with the gravel, and asking me to come.

Louisa carried letters also; one from a swain, a carpet weaver in Rouen. She was identified as Mademoiselle Jeanette Perrochet. She was an orphan, and carried a letter from the nuns of a convent who had brought her up, as a child.

Paul was Paul Wenskalski. He was illegitimate. His mother was French, but his father had been a chapman from Poland, who had promised her marriage, and then disappeared. I was ordered to be a little peremptory in my address to Paul; as if he was tolerated in the family only; and was looked down upon because of his unfortunate birth.

Upon the ship, in the privacy of Paul's cabin, we rehearsed our parts. Paul was endlessly patient with us; especially with Louisa, who appeared to need his extra attention. On one occasion he took her on deck with him, so that they could be alone. I felt a strange pang in my heart as I watched them go. And then I steeled myself against personal reactions. We should all need all the histrionic skill we possessed to play our parts and not reveal our true identities, and our real errand. I began to guess how difficult this was going to be.

Yet I could not stop myself from thinking that upon this unknown journey into France, Paul would be with the woman he loved.

He would not reveal his attachment, or make his preference known. That was not his way. He was a man of honour in all departments of his life. But at least he would be near her, able to help and support her in our joint cause. Even such proximity to one in love, is a matter of gratitude and felicity.

I hoped that Louisa would return his regard by complying with his wishes. Of course she was still engaged to Charles. Nothing at the present could alter that. And yet sometimes I thought ... Her glance on Paul was warmer than required, her tone softer, her touch lingered when she had occasion to brush by his arm.

Heaven knows how things will turn out on this voyage and this journey, I told myself. I could not quell the fear and apprehension in my heart.

This passage was rough, the seas were choppy and the ship bucketed sharply. Louisa was soon overcome with *mal de mer*; but somehow I survived this malady. That night, I lay in my cabin alone and pondered the situation in which I found myself.

I had longed to experience all that life could bring against me; and life had obliged me with a variety and a sharpness of emotions and situations; of actions and reactions of love, betrayal, pain, longing and desire.

Physical love had overwhelmed me, and the unexpectedly wonderful sensations of physical passion had been mine. And so had despair, regret, awakening, illusions and disillusion. The whole gamut of human feelings had been mine in a comparatively short space of time. And the catalogue of my experiences was not yet over; of that I was sure.

I felt a deep regret at my final parting with Anthony. Regret that I did not feel more acutely the reality of our parting; regret that the love I had once borne him had not rekindled, and was now like lukewarm ashes in my heart and mind.

I remembered his farewell words to me. 'Return to me safely, my dearest girl, I beg of you. I let you go with deep reluctance, for I know full well the hazards of your course.

'Yet I know you are set upon this venture, and that you will not be satisfied unless you undertake it. Therefore, I salute you before you go, and assure you of my undying love and regard.'

He had kissed me fondly, and I had replied to the salute, feeling that his now unstinted devotion deserved at least this pledge of amity and understanding. Then he had squared his shoulders as I had stepped from his arms. I was surprised to find that tears, unbidden, and not allowed to fall, shone in his eyes.

I remembered also a scene I had witnessed, prior to our departure, again as I was about to descend the stairs, with my cloak over my arm.

Below me Anthony and Paul stood in conversation, again.

'I entrust her to you, Paul. She is the greatest treasure of my life,' Anthony was saying.

'My titles and money which once meant so much to me, for which at one time I was ready to go to the most extreme lengths to obtain, mean little to me now, compared with my wife.

'Guard her well. Bring her home to me safely. I love her beyond my own life, as you know. She is all I have, and I ask from life for nothing more than her safe return.'

I saw the earnest expression upon Paul's face as he regarded his cousin. 'Believe me, I will do everything possible to safeguard the one you speak of in every way,' he said.

'I know your devotion to her, and her well-being shall be a prime consideration with me.

'Yet do not take matters to heart so intently,' Paul advised Anthony. 'You are clearly fearing the worst and believing that adverse circumstances will assail us.

'But it is surely more than possible that this venture will go well. That we shall obtain success. That within a short space of time we shall be back in Beaufroy House again, with Charles Latham, our charge, safely home.

'Come, take an optimistic view of our chances. It is ill service to myself to be so pessimistic! Trust me to do all that is necessary at all times to...'

The voices of the two men died away, as they moved along the hallway towards the front door. Paul was already clad as a wheelwright. His tools were slung across his shoulder in an artisan's bag.

The next morning Captain Vicary bade us farewell; he was more civil now that his human cargo was about to be discharged. To my surprise he gave us all a small parcel of food and advised us: 'Go carefully, for France is in a ferment of military activity, and hardship. I would rather walk the plank than venture across this stricken country.' He saluted us, then turned away, as if he felt his duty was over and his obligations fulfilled.

It was now up to our small party to make our way, unassisted towards Paris. Guided by Paul we headed for an inn near to the waterways of Calais. This inn was also a trading-post and coaching-house. When we entered, we were told that the coach for Lille was due shortly. We asked for wine and fresh bread, and this was produced for us, promptly.

My spirits rose. We were clearly accepted for what we were; a party of relatives travelling inconspicuously together. There was a fire in the main room of the inn, and we thawed out our frozen bones in its glow. I dared to hope that this auspicious beginning would continue. Success might be ours more speedily than we had thought.

But to my dismay, Louisa herself spoilt this illusion. I had ordered the bread and wine sparingly, as a thrifty bourgeoise would. But suddenly, at the end of our repast, Louisa herself asked the potman to bring her more wine. 'And a flagon, please. I am thirsty and tired, and wish to enjoy this burgundy.'

Her clear, rather patrician voice with its Parisian accent rang out in the room of the inn. Several workmen drinking nearby glanced at us surreptitiously. Some whispered together. We became suddenly the unwelcome focus of attention from the French burghers. I felt a crimson flush dye my face, and I know my eyes flashed with indignant fire.

I reproved Louisa sharply, acting out my role of her mistress; and emphasizing her station as my maid. Paul reinforced my words, speaking in a broader accent, and chiding Louisa with trying to rise above her station, and ape the manners of her superiors.

The men watching laughed; clearly accepting the situation. Yet the whole incident left a feeling of unease within me. The journey would be doubly hard if Louisa had to be watched at every touch and turn.

She took our reproofs with ill grace. She followed us outside when the coach arrived, and accompanied us into the conveyance. Paul paid our tariffs from his pouch of coins, hidden in his workman's jerkin. We sat silent as the coach gathered speed and sped away.

During this journey, we were glad of our packed parcels of food. The coach was badly sprung and rattled with every stone encountered and crossed. We left the environs of Calais and the coast behind, and headed into the interior of France. The scenes of the countryside passed joltingly before our eyes.

There was no doubt that the war had struck an almost mortal blow to the French Republic. Men stood in idleness in the market towns; the farms seemed unattended, the factories closed. And there was no doubt also that the revolution had left a legacy of misery and debt. I felt grief as we travelled across a landscape stricken and neglected. The dilemma of the French people cast a shadow over my mind.

At Lille, where we were to spend the night, we entered the coaching inn, as the coachman directed. We asked for food and rooms for the night. I was told that I and my maid, Mademoiselle Perrochet, would be obliged to share.

We freshened ourselves after the long and cramped journey, and sat down to our evening meal of onion soup, and a platter of meat and vegetables. At once I noticed a change had come over Louisa.

She had been instructed to be unobtrusive and discreet; but now, since we had landed in France, it was as if a new and vaunting confidence had assailed her.

She began to talk in a loud voice, again asking openly for wine; again her voice and accent rang about the room. I asked her to quieten herself, dreading the consequences. She answered:

'But we are in France now. My own country. I cannot tell you how glad I am to be here. Glad to have left behind for ever that dreary England, and cold London and gloomy Beaufroy House. I am here, in my own country, a French woman again, an accepted person and not a foreigner. Potman, please bring me more wine!' And she took the flagon from his hands, and poured herself a generous measure.

At the end of the repast, a gentleman approached me, and engaged me in civil conversation. He appeared to me to be a notary, or other professional man, travelling towards Paris.

'Your maid, Madame,' he said, 'appears to be of aristocratic birth or inclination. Her intonation is aristocratic. Yet today, in France, this accent is frowned upon. Since the revolution the nobility has been in decline. Their ways of life and manners are not acceptable to the mass of people. I wonder therefore, about your maid. Can you enlighten me?'

I smiled at my questioner, and told him that she was an orphan, brought up by nuns in a convent in Paris. 'And as you know, m'sieur, many nuns are of aristocratic birth, and some of their mannerisms and modes of speech have descended off to my maid.

'But I will chide her, for I know her behaviour is out of place.' And I looked at Louisa who was talking to Paul, a filled glass of crimson wine in her hand.

At this moment, Paul escorted Louisa out of the inn. Later he told me that he had privately reproved her soundly for her behaviour. I went upstairs to my room. Some time later, Louisa came in.

To my dismay I smelled the wine upon her

breath, and her speech was slurred. Paul, I learned later, had thrown the flagon of wine away; but not before it had gone to Louisa's head, and had caused her to lose the control so necessary to our disguise, and our purposes.

I wondered at this new inclination of Louisa's. At home, in London, she had shown no inclination to be indebted to wine; she had drunk freely, it was true, but always with control and the observance of civilized behaviour.

Yet now ... I listened to her snoring breathing from the other bed. And doubt and uncertainty filled my already anxious and perplexed mind.

The next day we set off early, on the next part of our journey towards Amiens and the capital. Louisa was quieter; clearly the after-effects of the wine had thrown her into depression. She sat in surly silence in a corner of the carriage. The gentleman who had addressed me during the previous evening eyed her and myself with a calculating gaze.

During the whole of this day, Paul's behaviour was a great support and guide to myself. And to Louisa, had she allowed this. He entered his part wholeheartedly. Had I not known him in London, I would have believed his disguise.

He was truly the wheelwright, proud of his own small business. He was deferential to myself, as the member of the family who had entered the bourgeoisie; he was clumsily gallant and protective towards Louisa. Suddenly, after Charcuse, she seemed to awake, and her attitude changed.

She turned upon Paul the full force of her magnetic personality and considerable charms. At a halt near some woods, where hot chocolate was served from a wayside brasserie, she engaged him in ardent conversation, and even threaded her arm through his.

She turned her radiant face upwards to his, pressing herself to his side. I was surprised at the indignation and dismay which flooded through me at her forward action and uninhibited behaviour.

Yet Paul played up to her, using her advances as a further step in our disguise. Some men passengers on the coach eyed this dalliance with amusement; some women frowned. As we prepared to re-enter the coach I asked Louisa to desist from making herself conspicuous.

'But why should I hide my feelings?' she asked me with a bold and calculating glance. 'I like Paul. I more than like him. I have a deep affection for him. It gives me pleasure to arouse him. I love to see the gleam of response in his eyes.'

'But you are already affianced to Charles Latham,' I answered. 'And your behaviour is unseemly, as well as dangerous.'

'If I do not marry Charles, I shall marry

Paul,' Louisa told me dismissively. 'And your objections to my conduct do not carry any weight with me.

'For you yourself are attached to Paul, in spite of yourself. Yes, you yourself want his attention and his regard.

'You are married, it is true. But you are already half the way to falling into love with Paul.'

CHAPTER FIFTEEN

During this same day, the gentleman who had approached me before, came to sit beside me as I sat in the porchway of a cottage trading-post, where home-brewed wine was served to the travellers, and some elementary personal facilities were available.

He greeted me civilly, and asked me to accept a bowl of thin soup, as his guest. He himself held a small glass of wine, but he drank sparingly. We both watched the horses being watered and fed in a companionable, and on my part, reserved silence.

My new companion was a man of about forty; well set-up and fresh in complexion with naturally curling brown hair, and dark eyes. His hands were well cared for, and his clothes good in quality, though not fashionable. He began to speak to me as I sipped the soup.

'My name is Alain Norbert, and I am a resident of Paris. I have my own house in the village of Versailles. I am a widower without family. My wife died some years ago.

'I am a leather merchant in a good way of business, but I lack companionship, and sometimes my way of life seems solitary and unrewarding.

'I know you are a widow, Madame. May I ask that you will enlighten me as to the occupation of your late husband, and your present way of life?'

I was pleased to do so; for I had my story well prepared, and was ready for this kind of questioning. Monsieur Norbert heard me out in silence. He did not appear to doubt my account of myself in any way.

'You are to visit your sick mother in Paris. I have gathered so much from general conversation in the coach. May I suggest ... May I ask ... That if you find yourself in difficulties in Paris, concerning this illness of your parent, that you will consider calling upon myself, so that I can give you my aid?'

I was very surprised by this statement, and the sincere and cordial way in which it was delivered. I thanked Monsieur Norbert kindly, and replied that I expected to be extremely busy, but I would bear his offer in mind and seek his assistance, if this should be necessary at any time.

'I assure you I will do all possible to be your

champion in Paris, should you need me,' this gentleman told me. 'And since I have your interests at heart, Madame Mairan, may I utter a word of warning concerning your maid?

'I advise you not to put too great a trust upon her. She is jealous of you. Envious too. Two conditions which spring from greed and insecurity. I urge you to watch her closely, and not to place too great a reliance upon her.

'But as for the young man, Paul Wenskalski, your cousin, he is a worthy and reliable person, dedicated to your welfare. Oh I know he is not within your social class. But he cares for you deeply as a relation. You can trust him, but I cannot say the same for your maid.'

I thanked Monsieur Norbert for his interest and comment, which I believed were well meant. He now assisted me into the coach, and moved his position in the vehicle, so that he could come and sit beside me. I allowed this gesture without demur; though I knew that the other passengers observed this manoeuvre, and some sly remarks were made concerning it.

Yet I told myself that to have this sudden friendship on the part of Monsieur Norbert added to our disguise. For I knew that, on coach-journeys, many friendships were struck up, and even romances begun; later to be relinquished and severed.

I felt that Paul approved this acceptance on my part. But Louisa, as usual, remained uncommunicative and dour. I could tell that she was far from popular with the rest of those travelling on the coach. I only hoped that we could complete our journey without further revealing or damaging incident.

Her words concerning my feelings for Paul suddenly burned in my mind; and I know that my face flushed, as I contemplated what her accusation meant to me.

It was true, I had felt from the first an instant attraction to Paul; in the hallway, when we had first met, there had passed between us a long glance of recognition and liking. A strange bond had been sealed between us from the first.

And during the dark and difficult days of my life at Beaufroy House, when my marriage had crumbled about me, and had finally lay in ruins around my feet... During these times Paul had been like a beacon of hope to me; a shaft of consolation, a presence within my life who had given me comfort and support.

I had appreciated deeply his sterling qualities, and the discretion and reticence with which he had faced his position in our household; and in the lives of Anthony and myself. We had both valued him. We had both cared deeply for him in our own ways.

But now, now Louisa's taunting words had made me look afresh at my deeper and most secret feelings. Was it true that I was falling in love with Paul; that he had taken the place of Anthony as the lodestar in my life?

Yet, if this was true, this was no dramatic

and overwhelming passion; no sensation of dizzying intensity, no acceptance of wild commitment. This was a steady pulsing regard, which was growing in force every day. Yes, I admitted this fact. Each day that passed drew me more closely to Paul, and made my inclination towards him, and my esteem for him grow.

And yet, I remained convinced that he was deeply attracted to, and indeed, in love with Louisa. No doubt her recent unaccountable behaviour had shaken his regard; yet Paul was not one to falter under the unexpected moods of a beloved; he was not one to give up easily. Adverse circumstances would not take him unawares.

Also, I told myself, I was a married woman, still bound by my vows of allegiance to Anthony. And however disappointing my marriage had proved; however lacking it now was in closeness and harmony, yet the formal bond remained. This was not something which could be lightly put aside.

And now, after further hours of travelling, as the coach reached the environs of Paris, Monsieur Norbert engaged me in conversation again. 'You will see, as we approach the capital, that there is strong evidence of military activity.

'Troops are drilling in the market squares and the open fields. Guns are being assembled and transported. Horses groomed ready for their work.' He paused. 'There is no doubt that a new and formidable battle will soon commence.

'Napoleon, that militaristic hawk, is rumoured to be preparing to quit Elba. They say there is a brig in the Mediterranean ready for his escape, and that seasoned troops are massing in Provence.

'The Duke of Wellington, also has returned to the continent. Did you know this? Had this news reached Calais, where you live? There is no doubt that a conflict between these two field marshals will soon materialize. And we ourselves, in France, will be locked in direct conflict with England again.'

Although I had been aware of this circumstance, in general terms, yet to have the matter spelled out to me in detail confirmed my worse fears. Our mission and our quest would be all the more difficult to execute, in the climate of imminent hostility, and outright war.

The coach now halted at an inn of fair size close to a northern suburb of Paris. Here several passengers alighted, for their own carriages and servants awaited them, to take them to their destinations. I saw that the inn was called Le Coq d'Or, and that there were signs of warmth and comfort within.

The coachman called that a halt was arranged here, so that those journeying into Paris could refresh themselves. Paul and I entered the inn together, and he ordered for us a glass of hot nutmeg grog. Louisa was not in sight, for which I was glad, as I wished to speak to Paul in privacy, and alone.

There was an embrasure set in seasoned wood, and along this bench Paul and I sat together. I said in a whisper, to Paul:

'Will you please refresh my memory as to the circumstances concerning the hiding-place of Charles Latham. And inform me of the next steps we must take to effect his release.'

Paul drew on a pipe, which he hated, yet which gave him an artisan air, and the clouds of smoke discouraged idle conversation. He replied:

'My last sight of Charles was in the Paris apartment of the deceased family of Louisa de Courcy. But it was, of course, far too dangerous for him to remain there, and Louisa offered to take her injured friend to her late family's secluded château on the southern banks of the Seine.

'I myself arranged transport for them, in a small-holder's vegetable cart. But before I could see them depart, I was called away by courier to London. But Louisa assures me that the journey was made, and that Charles arrived safely at the de Courcy family's country home.'

Paul stopped, to refill his pipe. He sipped his wine and resumed:

'I believe Louisa's word, implicitly, of course ... And yet no trace of this château has so far been found.

'David Exeter, the first agent sent into France to bring Charles back to England, reported back to London that he could discover no trace of the Château Vallonne, which is the name of the de Courcy family's rural residence.

'Unfortunately as we know, the second agent, William Lansbury, was apprehended, tortured and slain. But not before—so we have recently learned—he had informed his courier friend that he had already searched for this château, but all his efforts had been in vain.

'So that it is up to us, Felicity, to locate the Château Vallonne and to make arrangements to take Charles into Paris. From there we can in due time effect his extradition to England. We shall receive aid to smuggle him back to British soil. One can only hope and pray that all will go well, and no impediments will arise to halt us in our course.'

'Can you not tell me,' I asked, 'the methods by which Charles will be taken back to England?'

'This I cannot do. It is never good for those engaged in agency affairs to know too much. What you do not know you cannot, under pressure reveal. But trust me, plans are laid. And you will see their unfolding in due time.'

It was at this moment that there was a disturbance at the back of the inn, and I saw that Louisa had entered with a flagon of wine in her hand, and that she was followed by the potman of the inn.

He was a tall, burly, well set up man of forceful and handsome countenance. He caught at Louisa's arm, and tried to detain her. 'What's the haste?' he cried. 'There is time for a kiss and a squeeze in the orchard before the coach leaves.

'You are not too proud are you, to make love with a potman? You're only a maid after all, you haven't occasion to put on airs and graces.'

Paul rose to his feet at once, and approached the serving man and Louisa. At Paul's scowl and air of authority, the potman released Louisa's elbow. He turned away with a surly frown and an air of impatience.

'Come outside, Louisa,' Paul said. 'There is a matter of importance to discuss.'

Louisa did not thank Paul for his intervention; she herself was flustered and rather inebriated, I thought. I observed her with unease, and a dreadful suspicion began to form in my mind.

'Where is the Château Vallonne, Louisa?' Paul asked directly. 'If my calculations are correct, it is within a few miles of this inn, Le Coq d'Or. And indeed, you yourself have told us as much, and have given us some rough directions.

'Yet where is the Château Vallonne actually situated? Is it within walking distance, or do we need a conveyance?'

'The historic Château Vallonne, my ancestral home, is but a few kilometres distance now,' Louisa informed us rather haughtily, I thought, though her affected mannerisms at this moment ill became her. 'It is difficult to describe the route,' she conceded. 'However, I will take you there,' she added, grudgingly, 'if you really wish to go.'

'Really wish to go!' repeated Paul in amazement. 'We have travelled across France in disguise for this very purpose! What is the matter, Louisa? I am at a loss to understand your words and your attitude!'

Louisa turned from us; I could not understand the expression upon her face. Then she added, 'We can walk to the château fairly easily, though the terrain is rough. I will lead you,' she continued more graciously. 'I will show you the way.'

It was now imperative that we removed our cases from the coach, as the conveyance was being prepared to undertake the last section of its route, into Paris.

Indeed, all the passengers had assembled outside the inn by this time, and were preparing to enter the conveyance preparatory to the coachman giving the word of command for departure.

I saw Monsieur Norbert looking at me anxiously. He seemed to wish to communicate with me; but there was no opportunity for this.

It was at this moment, that the potman from the inn approached us again, and again waylaid Louisa, clutching her arm, with a drunken and vicious leer.

'If you are not journeying on into Paris,' he cried. 'We can meet later, and drink together. I have a room in a cottage nearby, where I can entertain my friends. And you and I can be more than friends. We can spend a delirious night together...

'And if you please me, I will reward you. See, this bracelet shall be yours if you play your part!'

He was entirely and utterly inebriated; beyond sense and discretion. I saw the keeper of the inn advance towards him with disfavour and disapprobation upon his face.

But Louisa had turned to face her interlocutor. I saw her expression harden. She drew herself up to her full height. And then her words rang out, clearly in the air; reaching the ears of the watching passengers, now getting into the coach. Causing everyone to pause and to stare at her aghast.

For her words were: 'Unhand me at once. How dare you address me in this fashion?

'Do you know who I am? I am the Countess de Courcy of the Château Vallonne.

'I am a French aristocrat by birth and breeding. You are not fit to serve me, let alone to assault my person, or address me with lewd intention.

'Stand aside. My ancestors would have had you whipped. Apologize. And address me by my title ... The Countess de Courcy of the Château Vallonne...'

CHAPTER SIXTEEN

The passengers entered the coach swiftly; turning their faces from ourselves and the scene they had just witnessed. There was no doubt that Louisa was an ill omen in their sight.

No-one wished to be in proximity to someone who was so blatantly tempting fate. The passengers' austere and withdrawn glances told us their opinion of someone who could openly boast of being an aristocrat. They wished to have no part in this confession, and what was to come.

'France is a republic now, and there are no titles,' the innkeeper told Louisa sternly. 'My potman was wrong to approach you in such familiar fashion, but you had no right to repulse him in such degrading terms.

'Many aristocrats are dead, perished in the revolution, now safely and well over, I am glad to say,' the innkeeper continued. 'If their descendants remain, they will be advised to have the wit to keep silent, and not to flaunt old privileges and old feudal attitudes.

'All that is finished now, Mam'selle. You are not superior to anyone else, and the sooner you realize this the better.'

Paul intervened hastily, and I saw a sum of money change hands. The innkeeper departed, and the three of us turned our faces to the open road. The sooner we quitted the inn, the better, I assured myself. We set out upon our way.

We had left our luggage in a stable at the inn; I carried only a reticule, and Louisa a hessian bag. Paul still carried hidden, the tools of his trade.

I shall remember this journey as long as I live. We soon branched off the main road, directed by Louisa, into a narrow side lane. This we traversed for several miles.

The way was rutted and uneven; it was cold, the wind blew, and flurries of rain assailed us. All this I could have borne without complaint and with equanimity, had not a dreadful pall of doubt and suspicion filled my heart.

I saw that Paul also looked preoccupied and downcast. I cannot imagine that building materials or supplies were brought along this route to a château, I told myself. There must be another way, or the château ... Was it a castle in Spain, an unsubstantial myth in thin air? I glanced at Paul, and saw the same suspicions in his eyes.

Yet Louisa led us still onwards; and now the lane had become a mere walking track; sometimes it petered out altogether, and we had to push our way through briars and foliage. 'For God's sake, are you lost, Louisa?' asked Paul. But Louisa did not reply, but still walked ahead.

Yet now I noticed a slowing down of her steps, it seemed she was reluctant to go forward. It was as if her resolution failed her, and she did not wish to reach her journey's end. We both went ahead to walk by her side; but she ignored us; it was clear that some matter was grievously wrong.

We reached at last a clearing at the end of these woods; here was an open space with no trees above us and no thorns at our feet. The sky stretched to the distance over open pasture land and fields. In the foreground, a village nestled beneath a shallow hill.

Paul swung Louisa round to face him, and he cried, 'Where is the Château Vallonne? Where have you led us?'

We saw now a heap of broken stones strewn about this open clearing; there was rubble, smashed statuary, the remains of charred wood.

'This is the Château Vallonne,' Louisa answered. 'All that is left of it.

'It was sacked and destroyed by the rabble during the revolution. It was torn to the ground, looted, and burned. This is all that remains. This is the country home of the de Courcy family! Destroyed during the revolution. Never to be rebuilt again.'

'But surely you have not brought us here to emphasize the injustices to yourself and your family perpetrated by the revolutionary forces!' Paul cried. 'Where is Charles? What have you done with him? Is he alive? Louisa, answer me! Where is Charles Latham who was entrusted to your care?'

'You care more for him than for me,' she answered childishly. 'But do not despair. He is safe, and well hidden, and in good hands.'

'Or at least he was, when I last saw him.'

And she gestured with her hands towards an ancient and tumble-down cottage, which was situated on the edge of the ruined site. We saw that the place was occupied, for a thin plume of smoke arose like a signal, from the chimney of the roof.

*   *   *

So small and dilapidated was this cottage, that it merged into the devastated site of the vanished château like a fragment of the ruins themselves. Yet now I saw that a few hens clucked around the tiny garden, and a pig rooted in the undergrowth of shrubs and grass. Louisa now began to moved towards this sorry place; and Paul and I followed closely on her heels.

She did not knock at the tumble-down door, but opened it carefully. Inside, was one room, dark and odorous with occupation. We saw a tall elderly man brewing gruel in a black pot upon the open fire.

He seemed not surprised to see us; but took his cue from the sight of Louisa to accept us into his home. 'You have been a long time in coming,' he said ungraciously to Louisa. 'You promised me it would not take long. I did not know I was going to be inconvenienced for so great a time.'

'Kindly address me in a civil manner,' Louisa told him haughtily. 'You were well paid for your services. We owe you nothing. And I do not relish impertinence from inferiors.'

'Your name may be de Courcy,' replied the elderly man, with equal emphasis. 'But I am now as good as you, and what I did, I did as a favour, and not because I owed any debt to you or your name.'

Paul interrupted at this point. He addressed the countryman. 'We seek my friend who I now believe is hidden here in your cottage. Will you take us to him, please.'

'If she had asked civilly, it would have been done at once,' the old man said. 'This way.'

I had been looking around the cottage, but could see no possible hiding-place for anyone in this diminutive shack. The old man went to a corner and pulled aside the table upon which he had laid the utensils for his elementary meal.

He bent down and pulled a tattered rug from the floor. He lifted a large metal ring and revealed a trap-door. Into this underground cavern he indicated that we should descend.

Paul led the way. The steps were steep and narrow and we went down into a grey twilight or semi-darkness. Yet someone was in this underground byre, for we heard a rustling, and then saw, in the half-light, a man lying prone upon a bed of straw.

His dark hair was matted upon his brow. His face was deathly pale, his eyes shadowed with pain and suffering and hardship. Yet an indomitable light shone in his eyes, and he half rose upon the straw and held out his arms towards Paul.

Paul crossed the earth floor quickly, and clasped the injured man in a friendly embrace. They spoke swiftly, exchanging essential information. Paul then turned to me, and said, 'This is Charles Latham, found at last, though how he has survived in this place I do not know.'

I privately agreed. For it was clear that Charles Latham was desperately wounded, and that gangrene had set in upon his injured leg. The stench of this wound filled the underground cellar, and it was obvious, that left alone, he would not have had long to live.

During all these exchanges between the two men, Louisa had stood aside, but now she approached the injured Charles Latham, and attempted to take his hands into her own.

He allowed the embrace which followed; but it seemed to me that his greeting lacked enthusiasm, and indeed, he drew himself from her, and sank back at last upon the folded jacket which was his only pillow.

'I am sorry I had to leave you here,' she cried finally. 'But I had no alternative. Please believe me, Charles. I did what I thought was best. I regret the hardship and the distress which has been caused you!'

'Yet this is scarcely a château,' Charles answered. 'Had I known my destination, I would have begged for another lodging. You could not have done me a worse service than to have deceived me and brought me here.'

And now Paul acted swiftly, for it was clear that the injured man must be removed from this cavern without delay.

'I will go into Paris to the house in the Rue Mordeau,' Paul told Charles. Later I was to learn that this was a house owned by the Duke of Wellington, and placed at the service of his agents. Here they could bank upon safety, and from here seek their route back to England.

'Can you endure one more night in this place, Charles? I assure you it will not be longer. I will return with a conveyance to transport you away. Take heart, dear fellow. I shall return speedily with the help you require.'

We then left the injured man upon his bed; Louisa would have lingered, but Paul motioned her to follow us without waiting. Outside the hut Paul did not waste time with further enquiries and recriminations. He said:

'We must return to the inn, the Coq d'Or. I will take you two ladies there, and there you must spend one night.

'I myself will then speed into Paris and alert the other agents, so that we can rescue Charles. I will see you both tomorrow when this is done. Come, let us begin the journey back. There is no time to lose.'

And so we began the long journey back to the hostelry. If before the passage through the undergrowth and rough lanes had seemed interminable; now it seemed doubly hard, and the recollection of the plight of the injured man lay upon us all. When we finally reached the inn, Paul bade adieu. We watched him depart.

Although there was much I wished to say to Louisa, yet I agreed with Paul's unspoken stricture that now was not the time to indulge in censure and blame. Louisa and I entered the inn, and found that the innkeeper had a room available. He asked us grudgingly, if we would care to take an evening meal, and we agreed. He suggested that we should be seated, and brought us wine.

I was then greatly surprised to see Monsieur Alain Norbert enter the room; he bowed in civil fashion, and then hastened to speak to us. 'How glad I am to see you again,' he cried to myself. 'I did not enter the coach to proceed to Paris. I felt alarmed by your sudden departure, and feared that some harm had befallen you. So I have waited your return.'

He pressed more wine upon us, and I felt greatly touched by his concern. He asked that we might all dine together, and with this both Louisa and I agreed.

It was at this moment, that there was a disturbance at the door of the inn. By this time in the evening the main room of the tavern was crowded with travellers, and others seeking refreshment. Voices were strident, as patrons took spirits and discussed recent events. The room was hot from the fire. Yet suddenly the voices seemed to die away, and the room became cold and chill.

We saw that gendarmes had entered the inn, clad in their military-type uniforms, their halberds at the ready, their eyes cold and calculating, their mouths set in a grim line. Both Louisa and I watched the two men as they pushed their way through the crowd. To my surprise, they came in our direction, and finally stood before Louisa and myself.

We rose to our feet; everything else forgotten as we faced the emissaries of the civilian authorities. The elder of the two men, and clearly the superior in rank, began to address us. He said:

'Information has been laid against you. You frankly and openly admitted to being the Countess de Courcy, a woman wanted by the police.

'You are well known to be a sympathizer with the enemies of the French Republic. You are indeed half-English, and formerly resided in England for your education. You ape their ways and their aims. You are well known to be on their side, and to be a traitor to France.

'Indeed, I am informed that you have recently returned from England, which is why the police have not been able to apprehend you. In spite of our diligent search, you have evaded us. Until now.

'And in addition, you are charged with openly abusing a reservist member of the French police who works here in disguise as a potman. You have also stolen from him an object of value, namely, a gold bracelet.

'Madame, I am placing you under arrest. You will accompany us into custody, there to await trial for your infamy, your treason, and your crimes.'

And so saying the burly gendarmes stepped forward and pushed Louisa aside. Both men seized me by the arms, and held me motionless, before they began to drag me, swiftly, away.

There was uproar now in the room at the inn. Voices were raised in condemnation; in protest; with threats, with jeers and scolding comments. Monsieur Alain Norbert was brushed aside by the gendarmes, and fell to the ground. Louisa's hand flew to her face, and I saw her eyes dilated with shock and consternation.

Then she began to have hysterics. She screamed and fell to the floor. She beat with her heels upon the ground. She writhed and shrieked. Monsieur Norbert rose to his feet, and attempted to lift her up, and calm her.

In vain I protested to the gendarmes that I was not the Countess de Courcy. That this was a case of mistaken identity; that they were making a vast error. They did not hear; or did not heed me. They hauled me forcibly from the inn, out to a tumbril-style cart which was waiting outside. They hoisted me into this cart and sat beside me, holding me; while their driver whipped up the horses, and the conveyance was driven away.

'To where are you taking me?' I cried. 'What do you want with me?'

'You will learn,' was the answer. 'You will learn everything now.

'You will have time to repent of your crimes, and then you will be tried and sentenced.'

And the two men laughed, as if at some great joke not yet explained. And the younger of the gendarmes hit me sharply across the face with his open hand.

CHAPTER SEVENTEEN

The Fréjel Prison was situated in a northern suburb of Paris; I do not know the name of this district. I was never to know. But I saw the gaunt grey pile rise up before us at the end of the ride in the open cart.

Grilles barred the windows and doors. Sentries stood on guard. The very aspect of the place seemed to speak aloud that those who entered here, were never likely to leave. The huge metal doors opened with a clang; and closed behind us like a knell of doom. Inside, was stone and iron, and the overwhelming smell of human imprisonment and ill treatment.

I was thrown without any preamble into a cell containing about a dozen other women. They were of all ages and conditions; all ranks and stations in life. What their crimes had been, it proved difficult to discover.

A common condition of both despair and endurance lay over this dungeon, blanketing the prostrate and crouching figures with its own miasma. They stared at me aghast as I stumbled among them. Not from pity, I was later to discover; but from resentment that I would take up valuable space, and be one more problem to those already to be endured.

An elementary sluice ran at the far end of this cell, and the mattresses nearby were long since matted and sodden. Water ran down the walls, and bedewed the high, barred window. Several women were coughing; and others lay with spots of high fever upon their wasted cheeks.

Yet soon, in spite of these hard conditions a place was found for me; and some of the women addressed me in civil fashion; asking my name, and proffering their own. They eyed my sturdy clothes and my cloak with envy; for by this time many of the prisoners were dressed in rags.

After about three hours, food was brought to us. This was an unsavoury mess upon metal plates. Water was poured; into which the prisoners' crusts of bread were dipped. I was unable to eat, but sank back against one wall of the dungeon, contemplating my present position, and my future in this place.

For some reason I thought first of Louisa. Though I felt extremely vexed with her for her deception concerning the hiding-place of Charles Latham, yet her sorry state, when I had left her, was strongly present to my mind.

I did not doubt that her hysterics at the inn were also a manifestation of her emotion at our reaction to her duplicity, as well as to the shock of finding that I was arrested in her place. I wondered what her future would be, and where she would turn to, now. For though few words had been spoken between herself and Charles Latham, yet Charles's unuttered rejection of her had been plain. It was clear to my mind that their romance was over; and she had no future by his side.

And Paul, what of Paul? How could he discover my whereabouts when he returned to the inn?

The gaolers had informed no-one of where I

was to be taken. There were doubtless many prisons on the perimeter of Paris. How would anyone know to which gaol I had been abducted? How could Paul learn where I was? I myself did not know this prison's precise location or its name.

Darkness fell swiftly in this gloomy cell. Yet it seemed that few could sleep.

I myself lay still against the wall, overcome in my deepest heart by a longing for a familiar face and form. But it was not my husband, Anthony, I was yearning for. It was his cousin, Paul.

I cried his name soundlessly on the foetid air. Paul, Paul, come to me. Seek me out. Rescue me.

I long to see you. I crave for your presence. I love you, I love you, I cried.

Heaven alone knows what the future can be, if I ever leave this place alive, I told myself. But silently, in my extremity, at this moment, I acknowledge this truth. I admit my love. I accept it in my deepest heart. With no evasions, no half-truth, no excuses and no denials. I love you Paul, with an intense and burning devotion, with a long-lasting and undying flame. I admit my love, and know that after this, life for me will never be the same again.

Soon sleep fell upon some in this cell. They cried during their slumbers; snatches of recollection, treasured names. I remembered the early days of my love for my husband,

Anthony.

I remembered the wildness of my attraction to him; the dizzying heights of sensation and anticipation. The fancies, the imaginings, the eagerness for experience. All gone now, I told myself. All the imaginings of a young and inexperienced girl had vanished under the onslaughts of experience. Life had dealt me such severe blows that my love for Anthony had not survived.

And yet, in miraculous fashion, my capacity for love had endured. My capacity for dedication and commitment had survived. Yet this time my love had no aspect of the dramatic; there was no eager searching for experience to fill any empty place in heart, body or mind.

Rather, this time my love had flowered naturally; had matured with the passage of time. My love for Paul had filled my life gradually. And it held for me, I knew, a greater stability and a greater endurance than before.

I also fell asleep finally; in the dawn we stirred awkwardly, our bodies filled with pain, facing another agonizing, interminable day.

Food was brought to us by a young man in warder's uniform. He was tall and slim, and about him there hung surprisingly, an air of elegance, and refinement.

'That is Leonard,' one of the women confided to me. 'He is kinder than most, though he tries to hide it. But it is his nature.'

She dropped her voice. 'You see, he is not as other men are.'

'Not as other men are,' I repeated mystified. 'What can this imply, may I ask?'

'Oh there is no deformity,' my informant told me. 'But he does not lust after the women. You see, he prefers men.'

'Prefers men?' I repeated again. I had never heard of such a circumstance previously; and had not encountered it at any point in my life.

'Perhaps you do not have this condition in England,' my new-found friend said. 'But it is certainly known in France. And Greece. It came originally from the eastern countries, and has now gained hold. But Leonard is the only one to be so afflicted, here. The other gaolers all prefer women. And believe me, they can take their pick and get their fill.'

These words awoke a feeling of foreboding and apprehension within me. And it seemed that a new hazard had been added to my imprisonment in this bastille.

At around mid-day the doors of the cell were flung open and a gaoler cried: 'On your feet for the commandant. Stand up, show respect. Or it will be the worse for you.'

They hit at the recumbent women with their halberds, hauling the sick to their feet, and pushing the frail against the walls. Then the figure of a man filled the aperture of the doorway, and there was silence as this being drew all eyes.

He was a gross man of great size, with a vast belly overhanging his breeches and pushing through his linen shirt and jacket. He wore a three-cornered hat upon his head, and had black leather boots upon his feet and legs. He carried a many-thonged whip in his hand.

'So, which is the new arrival,' he said, as he advanced into the cell. 'But I have no need to ask. For the Countess de Courcy is clearly here for all to see.' And he pushed towards me and eyed me with a long calculating gaze.

I returned his gaze. I tried not to flinch. I held my head high and did not speak. For I had long since learned that to deny my identity meant that I was branded a coward who was disowning my name and my family. And to be considered a coward at this moment, was the last thing I wished to endure.

'Comely, very comely,' he said. 'And young too. I must admit I did not expect someone so fresh. And spirited. I can see that. But I like a little spirit. Not too much, but a little adds spice, like herbs to meat, or cinnamon to fruit.

'And talking of meat and fruit and herbs, Madame la Comtesse—will you do me the honour of dining with me this evening? In my quarters. Leonard will show you the way. At eight o'clock. Do not be late. And do not make other appointments. For you will not be returning to your cell, after our meal.'

There were hidden snickers of amusement at these words, from the underling gaolers who were waiting beside the door. But I fancied I saw a *frisson* of horror and revulsion pass across the ravaged faces of the women in the poisonous dungeon.

'God must aid you,' another woman said to me, when the men had gone. 'Call upon His name and His mercy to deliver you, for no human aid can reach you, once you have entered the quarters of Duclos, and you are alone with him.'

This was my own conclusion, now that I had seen the commandant, and listened to his words. But a deep perplexity settled upon me, as I sought in my mind for some way to evade the horrors which were so clearly to come.

Later that day, the door of the cell again opened, and we saw a woman standing in the doorway, scrutinizing us, and the conditions in which we lived.

I saw that she was tall, handsomely and broadly built; with a bold and high complexion and blonde hair worn high in the French pompadour.

She was fashionably dressed in brocade and velvet with a cloak of fur and ribbon. Her eyes picked me out, and she gazed at me with a hostile and penetrating stare.

She was clearly no prisoner, but was connected to someone in authority; and allowed to have her run of the prison. The door closed after her, swiftly, when she had gone.

'That was Madame Duclos,' someone said.

'She always comes to inspect the new arrivals, to see which her husband is going to deflower, that night.

'If they are old, she knows he will not be disloyal. But if they are young, she realizes full well what will be afoot.

'She is familiar with his ploys and his methods of action. He does not fool her. She keep a close watch upon him.'

For some reason this news did nothing to ease the foreboding which filled me. I had felt her malevolence directed towards me. It seemed that I had another enemy now to cope with; and yet another hazard to be countered and overcome.

At almost eight o'clock the handsome Leonard came for me, and escorted me from the cell. The other women watched me go. They looked at me with pity and sorrow. Yet as Leonard closed the door of the dungeon, I heard one woman say, 'At least she will be offered a decent meal.' Then the key turned in the lock, and Leonard and I were alone together in the long stone-flagged and metal-barred corridor.

He began to escort me down the long passage-way. Suddenly he spoke, and to my amazement I heard his voice in English, whisper:

'Do not betray any reaction to my words, or my presence. Behave as if you do not hear me. But listen carefully.

'Through our network we informed Paul that you are here, and he is stationed outside. We will devise some means to aid you, given time, though we do not yet know how.

'But take courage, we are with you. That is all I can say.

'I cannot help you in your interview with Commandant Duclos. No-one can. You must bear what awaits you, alone. But remember...' Then he cried more audibly, in French, as he pushed me roughly along the stony passage, and we passed another warder. 'You are lucky to have been signalled out for an evening with the commandant. Many women prisoners wish for this honour, and are denied.

'Be civil, and appreciative. For if you do not please the commandant, your body can be picked up from the Seine. For there is no trial here, no judge and no courts. Only the commandant's word and what he wishes. If you want to see another day, try to survive as best you can...'

And with this advice Leonard hustled me up to the door of the commandant's room. He knocked, and opened the door. He bowed to the commandant, and indicated myself. The next moment I was inside the room, and the door had closed, firmly, behind me.

CHAPTER EIGHTEEN

I saw that the commandant's private room had formerly been a surplus office, but this had been furnished as a salon and dining-room combined. Duclos had added chairs and a table; an escritoire, and a stained and worn *chaise-longue*.

The effect was incongruous and somehow sordid. Everything was spotted with use and scuffed with neglect. One or two ornaments added to the general atmosphere of unreality and almost theatricality. Yet there was nothing unreal about Duclos as he stood beside the table in the centre of the room.

He had changed his uniform into a more formal habit; I saw the dark blue of his coat, with the mustard-coloured frogs and braid. Now that he had removed his hat I saw that he was younger than I had thought. His cheeks had an almost port-wine flush, and his eyes were dark and calculating. His vast stomach still overhung his breeches; but his chest was broad in proportion, and his arms muscular. He was clearly a powerful man at the height of his strength. His eyes swept over me in anticipation, and he bowed his head.

He advanced across the room towards me. 'Welcome to my private quarters, Countess,' he said. 'I am honoured to have you as my guest for the evening meal.' And he put out his hand and drew me further into the room. He indicated the table before us which was already set with fruit, viands, and wine.

He watched me closely as he saw me regard the table, and the sumptuous meal already arrayed before us.

I had not eaten for three days. My last meal had been a cup of hot chocolate and a fragment of dark bread at the inn, before Paul, Louisa and I had set out through the woods, to attempt to find Louisa's château.

Since then I had not been able to touch the prison food; nor had I drunk the water. I was weak with longing for some acceptable sustenance. My eyes took in the repast with a kind of disbelief, while Duclos continued to watch me as a poacher will watch a snared animal in a trap.

I saw roasted lamb and beef; assorted vegetables, with gravies, sauces, cheeses, cakes and wine. There was a gigantic tart, glazed with sugar and laced with cream. Wine stood in carafes, and the goblets were already full. Duclos laughed a little as he regarded the feast, seeing the table and its setting through my eyes.

I realized that this was part of his seduction scene. He would bring the woman of his choice here, and offer her first this bounty to quell her hunger and thirst. And then ... What his next ploy was, I could not even guess, for he had again taken my hands, and had drawn me with strong fingers to the table to take a seat there, by his side.

I could not eat or drink. Some inner compulsion stayed me. My stomach rebelled of its own accord at the richness of the spread before me. Cramps shook me, a bout of nausea assailed me. Duclos heaped my plate with viands, but they remained untouched.

'So you have lost your appetite,' Duclos said, as he speared a large piece of mutton and raised it, dripping fat, to his lips. 'But you should eat, to preserve your strength. It will be a long night, and I do not like fainting misses or ladies who are too fragile for my purposes. Eat up, or at least drink.' And he proffered me an overfull goblet of wine, but the liquid spilled upon the cloth and ran down the leg of the table.

Duclos continued to eat, cramming the victuals into his face. Finally he said, 'Let me make the position plain, since you do not respond to my overtures, and fail to rise to the honour being granted you, of dining with the commandant of the prison.

'This is no scene of violence. Or at least, not at first. I am a man of refinement and honourable impulses. I enjoy high living and polished manners and behaviour. You, as a countess, will know what I am talking about. I am no rascal seducing a chambermaid. This is cultivated society, and our behaviour will match the occasion.'

He drank deeply and the wine spilled down his chin. He wiped his flushed face with the back of his hand. He wiped his nose between his fingers.

Still I did not answer. There seemed to be no reply to these words. He waited for me to speak, then continued, 'After the meal I like and require a voluntary surrender on the part of my lady guest.

'I like to enjoy a willing act of love, granted to me from gratitude, honour and appreciation. But if these attributes are not vouchsafed to me, and if my guest remains obdurate, then ... violence will be applied. And this is no small matter, since my strength is vast, and can be used to unusual effect upon a lady unwilling to accept the honour I am giving her. I must tell you some ladies are foolish, and do not appreciate the danger they place themselves in. Many are injured. Some do not survive.'

Duclos eyed me again, then helped himself to fruit and cheese. I saw him crack a nut in a silver utensil. The shell fell upon the table, the kernel, he clamped between his teeth.

'So what is it to be, then?' he asked me. 'Surrender or force?'

I eyed the loathsome man before me; seeing his perverted nature that required his female victims to abase themselves before him, before he robbed them of their honour.

This seemed to me to be so much worse than

rape or carnal despoliation. For Duclos was asking from his victims their self-respect, and the denial of their principles. I did not doubt but that, when their surrender had been effected, gross and violent measures would be taken against them.

'Well, be it upon your own head,' Duclos told me finally. 'Though I am disappointed in you, Countess. Although to have so high a titled lady brought to heel and the obedience of my hand, will add a further spice and delight to my pleasures I have not so far experienced.' And Duclos put out his giant hand and ripped the sleeve and shoulder from the bodice of my dress.

I sprang to my feet. My detestation of the man before me overwhelmed me. Yet I knew I could not take flight; I knew that my physical resistance to him would be useless, and would merely inflame his perverted passion. Yet I stood before him in defiance; I know that hatred blazed upon my face. I know that I stood like a ramrod, and every atom of my physical body opposed him. And every atom of my mind and spirit opposed him too.

Duclos sighed with disappointment. 'I was told that the aristocracy were loose in their living. That lovemaking was as common to them as taking bread. It seems that someone is lying to me. And that someone is you.'

Duclos now rose to his feet and advanced towards me as I backed away. I knew that when the far wall of the room was reached I had no bolt-hole; there was no way back or forward. Again he reached out, and this time touched my bare flesh. I lashed out at him in loathing and vengeance. And I know the detestation of him was patent upon my face, and in the force with which I assaulted his body, raining blows upon him with my clenched fists, and trying to hold him at bay. He held me at arm's length at last, and laughed.

His laughter rang out around the room like a roll of thunder, I heard the sound echo in the corridor outside; I saw his giant belly shudder with his merriment. And then, at this moment, the door of the room was flung open and a woman stood on the threshold, observing the scene.

This was the same woman who had earlier come to inspect me when I was imprisoned in the cell; this was the woman known as Madame Duclos. She stood quite still and inspected the scene before her: the room, and the participants; my torn dress, the violence, the ruined table, the spilled wine. And Duclos still laughing with his face flushed, and his clothing awry from the violence of my blows.

I saw that she was still elaborately dressed in brocade and silk, with ribbons and pearls. Her pompadour was elegantly formed afresh, and supported by jewelled combs and clips. Clearly, Duclos made a good living by running this gaol: clearly there were many pickings from the misery of the inmates of this prison. I saw Madame Duclos's expression harden as she stared at her husband and myself. And then she advanced into the room.

'So I have caught you at last,' she said to Duclos. 'Emil Duclos, I have caught you red-handed.

'I have suspected you for months. Years even, but have never been able to pin you down. I have never been able to catch you red-handed at your adultery, at your betrayal of me and your marriage vows.

'What will the priest say? Your sons and your mother? You have betrayed your faith as a good Catholic. You have set me at naught, when I brought you my dowry! You are an unfaithful husband, and you deserve the censure you will receive!'

I gazed at Madame Duclos in amazement. For it was clear to me that any cruelty it had been her husband's intention to inflict upon any inmate of this prison, was as naught to her, compared with his act of adultery. His only fault in her eyes was his deception of her, and his infidelity behind her back.

Yet even as I realized this fact, she strode into the room with a tiger's gait, and raised a large brocade bag she carried in her hand. And with this she assaulted her husband, raining yet further blows upon him, lacerating his head, bruising his shoulders, and butting his gross stomach.

His cries of pain and surprise rang in the air. My blows had not hurt him. They had been part of his act of degradation and rape; but his wife's violence overcame him; he shuddered and covered his face with his hands.

They began to shout at each other, both speaking at once, their testimonies incoherent. Explanations, accusations, protestations rang in the air, but I did not heed them. The door of the room was open, and I turned tail and fled from the room.

I was in one of the long wide stone corridors which were such a feature of this prison. I did not know which way to run, I chose the way from which fresh air seemed to come, and sped along the flagged path. And then I saw a warder advancing towards me.

A cry of despair came from my lips; and then my fears were eased. For hastening towards me, through the gloom of this underground place, was the slim and elegant figure of Leonard. He reached me in a moment, and barred my way. But when he spoke his voice was strict and his manner hostile. And my newly found hope died away.

* * *

His words came to me through clenched teeth. 'Run down the corridor to your left, towards the main entrance.' And with these words Leonard made a grab at me, as if to detain me against my will.

I avoided him, and ran along the passageway in the direction he had indicated. At the far end, I saw another gaoler appear.

Leonard came up behind me, caught me, and grappled with me. 'God's honour, but you are fierce!' he cried. 'But you will not escape while I am on duty.' And he seized the bunch of cell keys which he wore on a leather thong around his waist, and raised this lethal weapon above his head.

'God forgive me for what I am going to do,' I heard him whisper. And then he brought the keys down upon my head and shoulder with all the force of his thin and wiry frame.

Yet with not all his force; with not all the malevolence he was expressing before the approaching other warder. In some way, by some sleight of hand, the terrifying bunch of keys escaped my skull and my skin, and fell against his own outstretched arm.

I had the wit to fall to the ground, and indeed, the impact of the keys had been formidable; though not disabling. I lay still, and tried to quieten my beating heart. I closed my eyes.

Leonard bent over me. 'She fought me, the vixen, and I was obliged to down her. This aristocratic scum show no respect and have no manners. But she will not escape, now.'

'Is she dead?' the other warder asked.

Leonard felt my skin and put for a brief

moment his hand over my heart. 'Not entirely, chief-warder. But nearly. She has almost breathed her last.'

'Just as I thought. As you say, she will not escape, now. Take her outside to the courtyard. She can be transported to the charnel-house with the others. The cart is due to move off in the morning. She is one the less. Good riddance to bad trash. You have served the republic well.'

I heard the warder-in-charge prepare to move away. And then he turned again and spoke to Leonard.

'There is blood on the stone-flags from the wound in her head. And you have got some on your arm!' He laughed. 'For all your appearance, Leonard, you do not know your own strength! Get the blood wiped up at once. As you know, the commandant does not like blood in the corridors. It offends his aesthetic taste. He reserves blood-letting for the privacy of the cells...'

The chief-gaoler laughed at his own joke; and Leonard joined in. Then footsteps moved away, growing fainter as the man walked from us, down the long corridor.

Without a word, Leonard gathered me up in his arms, and held me against his chest. He was surprisingly strong for so elegant a man. I knew that the blood which had fallen in the corridor had been Leonard's own. Yet guessed that he would discount this, and that he could hold his own among the rough and tumble of life in this cruel prison.

He began to walk swiftly along the corridor, to what I surmised would be the rear-door of the bastille. I had the wit to lie motionless in his arms, hardly to breathe, and to appear insensible.

The fresh air of the outer courtyard hit me like a blow in the face. It was sharp and cold, after the oppressive, foetid atmosphere of the prison. Above me, I glimpsed the brilliance of stars, and clouds moving in a dark blue sky. Leonard still carried me easily towards a row of buildings flanking the courtyard. He opened one door, and we went inside.

He whispered, his lips scarcely moving, 'For what I am forced to do, you must forgive me. But I have no alternative. There is no route out of this prison, save this.

'Do not move. Continue to lie still, feigning death or serious injury. And maintain this before those you will now encounter. Those truly dead or injured, who are on their way to their final destination. Which is the charnel-house maintained apart from the prison.'

He passed through another room, and a short corridor, and came at last to a final cell. And in this stood a grim open coach, with the shafts ready for the horses; with the bridles prepared, with the big doors of the outhouse already on the latch as if for imminent departure.

Leonard raised me up without ceremony and thrust me into the interior of this tumbril. I landed upon the occupants who were already there.

Even now, after this time, as I write this chronicle, I can remember the pitiable condition of those within this desperate conveyance.

Some were already dead. Some expiring. Others seriously ill or wounded. Some had lost their reason. Others had lost hope, and were filled with despair.

Yet they showed me kindness. Broken bones were moved aside for me; emaciated arms touched me with a kind of mute sympathy and conjoining. Voices murmured words of comfort and consolation. Tears ran involuntarily from my eyes, and soiled rags wiped these away.

I learned later that these sorry inmates were those prisoners who were too near to death to respond to torture or ill-treatment. Many also, had given Duclos all they possessed in the world, through blackmail, and promise of release. When they were penniless, they were discarded from their cells, to make way for others who could receive the same treatment. Death was at least a relief to their disillusioned and terrified eyes.

I do not know whether I fell asleep naturally, in this tumbril, or whether the blow on my head and shoulder brought about a condition of unconsciousness. I only know that all further recollection of night in this cell of departure was wiped from my mind and my consciousness. I only know that I passed the next hours inert and without sensation or memory of my plight.

Yet I woke once, and saw in a flash the girl I had been only so short a time ago. I remembered my craving for experience, my longing to front and feel with all my senses all that life itself could hurl against me.

I had felt enough, and more than enough, of that I was sure. But like a revelation to me in the darkness of this dreadful place, I realized that it is not experience itself that is so vital to our lives; but our own reactions to these experiences.

Our own reactions to the onslaughts of life are vital to our growth and maturity. These expressions of our personalities in action are the turning blades in our hearts, and are vital both to our present and our future. Without our endurance and response, life itself must wither on the bough and grow stale.

I fell asleep again, or lapsed into unconsciousness instantly. When I awoke at dawn—for the light was filtering into this cell through the smeared windows—I found that I was resting within the embrace of an elderly woman emaciated from starvation. Her stick-like arms supported me against her breast.

But the horses were being backed into the

shafts of the cart, and the tackle was being fitted and hauled into place. And within a short space of time the coachman mounted his seat and took his whip in his hand.

The doors of the cell were opened, and light flooded into the gloom. He touched the horses lightly, and the tumbril began to move from the stable into the air of the prison courtyard, outside.

I heard, rather than saw the huge prison gates open for the tumbril to enter the street outside. I had the wit to lie inert. I felt the jolt of the vehicle as we passed over the cobbled courtyard. And then voices reached my ears from the crowds, waiting for the tumbril, outside.

CHAPTER NINETEEN

This was not a hostile crowd, as I had expected. There were no cries of derision, of hatred or seeking of vengeance. This was a silent throng, awaiting in the cold light of the dawn for the tumbril to emerge. A faint murmur arose from those assembled outside the prison walls. To my ears, it sounded like a muffled prayer.

Later, I was to learn that this crowd of relatives and friends of the prisoners in the Fréjel gaol, assembled several times a week, when the wagon was due to emerge, carting away to their final destination those whom the prison system had decided to discard.

The waiting horde pressed forward close to the tumbril, peering at those unfortunates within. If their own relative or beloved person was not in this cart... Then there was hope. He or she was still alive, inside. A frail consolation, yet it was better than to see the loved one destined for the final, unthinkable end.

Two guards accompanied this tumbril, marching one each side of the doomed conveyance. They pushed the thronging crowd back roughly, yet they could not still the human noise. For now the hub-bub had increased in volume. Names rang on the air as relatives were recognized. Those who had recognized no-one vented their miseries and relief to those overcome with horror and despair, as they saw the immediate plight of their friends; as they accepted the inevitability of the end.

The tumbril turned a corner; it was now out of sight of the prison. I now felt, rather than saw, an unusual circumstance taking place.

A fracas had broken out on the pavement. There was fighting, jostling, blows. Some ugly scene had erupted nearby, and the guards were alerted. They did not wish any uninhibited violence to reach the prisoners, or to hinder the progress of the cart.

The guards left the tumbril, and ran to the scene of the disturbance. Immediately, I heard a strong voice ring out, raised high in remonstration. 'Coachman! Hi, coachman! Halt. Rein your horses. The wheel of your vehicle is loose! Look, the wheel is nearly off its staple. Wait! Look at your right wheel. For God's sake, the hub is falling apart.'

I opened my eyes a little, and saw, amid the throng, a young working-man in a rough leather jerkin, holding a bunch of tools aloft.

'I am a wheelwright,' he cried. 'Look, examine my tools. You will soon discern my trade. Let me tighten the flanges and make the wheel secure. You cannot progress further with the right wheel in such a sorry state.'

The coachman drew in the horses, and turned to examine the young man, and to peer at the rear wheel. 'God above, the scallions in the prison workshop skimp their work, and cause me endless trouble. I have complained repeatedly about their incompetence. Tighten the bolts then, and be swift about it! It is a public service you are doing, for I must get to my destination without delay, under penance of severe reprisals to myself.'

Paul pushed through the crowd to the side of the tumbril. He glanced at no-one. He was apparently not concerned about the prisoners within the conveyance. He bent his head to the wheel, and I saw his tools in his strong and capable hands.

He began to turn with force the bolts of the wheel. The crowd murmured. I saw the sweat stand upon Paul's desperate and anguished face. And then, in one movement, the entire wheel of the coach came off; the tumbril spilled to one side, and the contents of the cart—the prisoners who were destined for extinction—were spilled upon the roadway of this Paris street.

At once the crowd sprang forward. The guards were alerted, and ran towards the tumbril, but too late. Relatives seized the hands of relative. Those too infirm to move of their own accord, were half dragged, half carried to the side of the road. Those who had already expired, were lifted from the ground, to be carried away to a decent and honourable burial.

There was tumult and chaos; the horses reared, the timbers of the tumbril collapsed with the impact of the coach upon the stony road. Men and women fled in all directions, dragging or hauling their companions away. The guards cursed, pursuing, but in vain. Within a short space of time the coachman was alone; his horses panicking, and his tumbril a mass of broken wood behind him.

Paul had seized my hand, early, and had dragged me after him across the road, through the crowd, and into a side alley. He ran down this aperture with all speed, using all his strength, dragging me after him, without respite, and seemingly without mercy.

I stumbled after him as best I could, my

lungs bursting with the exertion, my limbs faltering from weakness and disuse. I heard my breath on the air, I fell, I was dragged up. And yet still we moved forward, still we ran down anonymous streets. Still we continued to put distance from the prison and the tumbril between us. Paul halted at last beneath an archway in an empty street. He allowed us both a moment's rest. And so we stood, and faced one another.

I knew that I was filthy from my experiences in the prison and the charnel-cart; I knew that the odours of those places clung to me still. My hair was in disarray. My clothing torn. And my shoulder and the upper part of my bosom were still bare from the onslaught which Duclos had made upon me.

Paul now took off his leather jerkin, and placed it around my shoulders. And at the touch of his hands upon me, it was as if the floodgates of emotion and realization broke within me, and I fell into his arms, calling desperately, his name.

I know that tears ran down my face, and my body shook with the climacteric of my emotion. I heard my voice on the cold still, morning air; but I do not know to this day the precise words that were said.

I know that I poured out to him the force and reality of my love. The strength of my commitment to him, the depth and intensity of my attachment.

I know that I took him into my arms, raising my arms to reach his shoulders, and hold him to me. I heard myself finishing my vital confession:

'And all through my time spent in the Fréjel Prison, it was the memory of you and you alone which kept me sane and caused my hope not to die.

'I loved you. I believed in you. I had the conviction that you would come to me. The memory of you and you alone possessed me. No-one else. You were my lifeline and my lodestar. You became then, and you now remain, the dominant being in my life. God bless you. Accept my love. For I have nothing else, at this moment, to give you.'

Paul held me close to him during the torrent of my emotion. He smoothed my hair, and with his fingers, tender and gentle, wiped away my tears. I felt his manly frame deeply affected by our proximity. I know that he too, was overcome with emotion, though he spoke no word. Finally, he drew my arms from his shoulders, and held me away from him.

He spoke at last. 'I shall always remember your confession of love, and your pledge of commitment. Believe me, you have my love in return, and my deep and intense and permanent attachment to you.

'I have loved you for a long time. Since the first time we met in the hallway of Beaufroy House. Do you remember? When I was garbed as a mendicant, and you offered me shelter and food. I have loved you without ceasing, and yet, of honour and necessity that love has had to be hid.

'You are a married woman, Felicity. And what is more, you are the wife of Anthony Lycett, my cousin, and one to whom I owe respect and allegiance.

'He is not only my relative, but my commanding officer, and a man who has shown me nothing but kindness, and by whom I am honoured with a whole-hearted trust.

'You and I have acknowledged our love. Time, I know, will preserve it. But it can have no expression in our lives.

'You must return to Anthony, and take up your life with him, as before. For he too loves you with a deep love which has brought enormous pleasure and benefits to his life.'

He put out his hand, and raised my face to his. He bent his head, and laid his lips upon mine.

I realized that where we stood, beneath the archway of this bridge in this Paris back-street, it had begun to rain. Rain drops fell upon us. Yet still we seemed reluctant to part, reluctant to end this moment of intense communion. It was as if we both knew that this moment of closeness was unique, and would never return.

'What of Louisa?' I asked finally, as I drew apart. Paul seemed surprised by my question.

'But surely you knew that Louisa was never

more to me than an object entrusted to my care by the Duke? I had no personal feelings for her, save pity in her plight, and a desire to fulfil my charge towards her.

'And you yourself asked me to befriend her, and this I did to please you. But beyond this, believe me, I have felt nothing for her. And indeed, cannot understand the question, or your concern.

'Her own actions have ruined any respect or feelings of friendship for her. She has been her own worst enemy, through her misguided behaviour.'

And then Paul, without more ado, seized my hand again and set off running, dragging me behind him. 'The rue Mordeau is nearby,' he said. 'I have been guiding you there steadily. Only a little way now, and we shall be safe.'

And he continued to drag me through the Paris streets, as the rain beat upon us, and Paris awoke to another day.

* * *

The house in the rue Mordeau was behind the façade of a cobbler's shop. The tradesman was already at work; he nodded briefly to Paul who escorted me through the shop premises to the back of the property. Here a staircase rose to the upper floors. The tap of the cobbler's hammer followed us as we mounted the stairs.

These were the premises owned by the Duke

of Wellington, to be a haven of safety for his agents in the French capital. The accommodation was spartan but clean; clearly these quarters were more offices and staging-posts than places of rest. There were elementary facilities for daily living; truckle beds and washing facilities. But there were notices everywhere advising caution, and that no trace of human occupation of these attics must be revealed to the world outside.

I washed and made a basic toilet. Even to comb my matted hair was something, and to sponge my aching limbs. I was provided with a jacket and a loose and anonymous cloak, with a hood, to cover my clothes and my person. I guessed that soon we must move from the comparative safety of this hidden place.

Paul brought me food. Croissants, black damson preserve, slices of sausage, and a flagon of wine. I could scarcely eat, due to my long period without food of any kind; but Paul insisted. He stood over me and watched me as I began to taste the provisions. And soon my appetite returned, and I ate with relish; feeling strength flow again into my limbs, and feeling also both my resolution and my courage being reinforced.

'What is our next step, Paul?' I asked finally. But Paul replied, 'I cannot tell you. You know already that agents do not reveal information prior to action. Trust me. We will be on our way soon. And we shall meet Anthony.

Anthony is due to join us at the climax of our mission. And so you will both be reunited before too long.'

He turned from me abruptly as he uttered those last words. Tears came into my eyes, but when I had recovered my composure, Paul had gone.

I now discovered that Charles Latham was already ensconced in this house. His wounded leg had received medical treatment, for one of the agents was a trained doctor. He also had been fed, and given the necessary attention to his person. I saw that he was a handsome man, with chestnut hair and hazel eyes, and a tall and lithe figure. I liked him immediately, and he seemed to return my regard. Finally, I said to him:

'What of Louisa? Will she be found and taken to England with us? What will be her fate?'

I saw a shadow fall across his face. 'I loved her, it is true, and I believed I had her love. Yet her actions towards me reveal that her principal emotion was not love, but pride.

'It was pride which made her keep from the world the fact that her château had been destroyed, and was nothing but a heap of rubble. It was pride which made her take me there, and condemn me to weeks as a prisoner in an underground animal stye.

'During this time, my love, before so strong, entirely died. I have no feelings left for her. I certainly do not want to see her again.

'She is a French national,' he added. 'Her life and future must be here, in France. We have done all we can for her. We can do no more.'

Charles changed the subject swiftly. 'Napoleon has escaped from Elba and has landed at Antibes,' he said. 'The veteran troops have rallied to him, and France is now preparing for total war.

'But the Duke of Wellington has long been prepared for this. A battle will shortly be joined, the precise location of which is unknown. But this battle will undoubtedly settle the fate of both France and England, and without doubt of Europe, for many decades to come.'

A chill smote my heart at these words; and I guessed that these circumstances would add to the difficulties of our escape. And indeed, these fears proved true. For later in the day the cobbler who worked downstairs came to see Paul.

'Two gendarmes are patrolling the street. And a posse of military have passed along the rue Mordeau only recently,' he said.

'This is unusual. I do not like it. I pray you all to go. At once. If my shop is raided, and you are discovered ... You know what it will mean for me. Death, but torture first. I beg you to be on your way, without delay.'

'At nightfall,' Paul answered. 'It is already planned.' But the other agents, including

Charles Latham, were, undercover, speedily moved away.

At dusk, Paul and I quitted the cobbler's premises, and walked swiftly together through the streets of Paris, towards the Seine. Finally, we saw the river before us, a long strand of silver reflecting the stars.

We moved rapidly along the quay, away from the more ornamental reaches of the waterway. Finally, we came to an area thick with commercial traffic. Long barges lined this dockside, ready to set sail in the morning. We heard the water slapping at the sides of these commercial crafts; and the *patois* of bargemen's voices could be clearly understood.

At one of the barges, long, shuttered, with its cargo battened down ready to sail, Paul halted. There was a narrow wooden landing-stage, and this we crossed to the deck of the vessel. I felt the barge move underneath our feet. A strong smell of metal filling the air. I heard a man's voice whisper my name. And my husband, Anthony, stepped from the shadows beside the hold.

He took me in his arms. I felt his passion rise within him, and threaten to overpower him, as he held me close. He rained kisses upon my face, my hair, and my throat. He murmured my name, as he gripped me in an overwhelming embrace. It seemed that he would never be satisfied by my proximity; that he could never bring himself to let me go.

Paul himself halted this embrace, and indicated that we should go below. And so Anthony preceded us into the nether regions of this barge; into the cabin where a lamp hung from the ceiling, and Charles Latham already lay in a bunk, his leg bandaged, and his body covered with a blanket of Flemish design.

It was at this moment that we heard the sound of footsteps on the quay above us, and cries of military command in the French language. We were at once alerted, and Anthony himself went to the companionway. We saw him mount the stairway to the deck.

I could not help but follow him, to observe what was amiss. And so I saw the two men on the wharfside, about to board the barge. They were in French military uniform, and had drawn swords. It was clear that it was their intention to commandeer this craft, and to prevent its sailing. There was no doubt we should all be taken prisoner, forthwith.

At once Anthony stepped forward. He was dressed in some anonymous garb, that seemed to blend into the darkness and the shadows of the boat and the dockside. But he had a sword in his hand. And there was no doubting his determination to resist any delaying in our sailing, or any further attempt to halt us in our course.

He stepped off the barge onto the quayside. He called to Paul, 'Cast off! Tell the captain to make way. Do not await my return. That is a direct order. Obey!' Then he stood his ground and faced the two men before him.

Paul, by my side, did not comply. He gave no orders, though I knew the bargeman was exactly ready for sailing. On no account would we leave Anthony on French soil, while his sacrifice made our safety possible. We watched. Yet it was only a moment in time.

For a swift battle with the poignards of the French military men took place; yet it was two to one. Paul now ran swiftly to the quayside to assist Anthony, but he was unarmed. We saw one of the poignards strike Anthony in the chest. We heard the blade smite the breast bone; we saw the blood spurt and colour his jerkin with darkness. And then he stumbled and fell, and was caught in Paul's outstretched arms.

The French soldiers stood back. One was appalled. He cried to his companion, 'But we were instructed to take them prisoner only. Not to kill.

'They are useless to the French cause dead. They hold precious information, and it is information our officers seek. You have overstepped the bounds of command. Let us out of here, fast.'

The two men turned tail and ran down the quay; I heard distantly, one cry, 'We must inform our command that they had already left. Keep silent about the wounding. Behave as if it had never taken place.' I heard their footsteps diminish, and then there was silence.

Paul carried the inert form of Anthony on board the barge. The bargeman, without more ado, cast off, and the vessel moved away from the quay. Paul laid Anthony upon the deck, and I fetched a blanket to cover him. Paul stripped open Anthony's jacket and attempted to stay the flow of blood from the wound.

I knew now that the wound was grievous. The poignard had shattered the breastbone, and penetrated within. In spite of Paul's efforts, blood seeped steadily from the laceration. I saw Anthony's eyes close, and his colour receded. His hands fell loosely from my grasp, and he sank heavily within the circle of my arms.

He spoke at last. 'You did all you could, Paul. No man could have done more. But listen to me intently, both of you. I must speak to you frankly before it is too late.'

There was a rush of air over us, as the barge gained the centre of the Seine, and left the shelter of the harbour. I saw the tall buildings on either banks of the river, saw distant trees, a bridge, and Parisians walking. We waited desperately for Anthony to resume.

'Do not think I was not aware of what has happened to you both. I saw the signs of your falling in love long before either of you thought of it, or admitted it to your consciousness. I saw the portents and possibilities, before these entered your minds. And now I can feel the flowering of your love, and that you have found one another, and come together.'

He raised his hand to quell us, as we both began to speak at once, and to remonstrate with him. 'Oh, do not misunderstand me. I do not accuse you of infidelity or deception. I would not be so misguided. But I can feel that you have confessed your love, and knowing you both, I can judge that you have told one another you must retract your admission, and in the future, draw apart.'

I saw a haemorrhage start from his lips. Paul gently wiped Anthony's mouth. He resumed:

'Paul, I want you to know that when I charged you to take care of Felicity for my sake, that I knew of your love for her. And that you would protect her, for your sake, as well as my own.

'Thank you, Felicity, for the happiness you have brought into my life. I behaved towards you unworthily, on several occasions. Say that you forgive me for these incidents, before I must leave you, and depart.'

'There is nothing to forgive,' I cried. 'The incidents are long over and forgotten. And your personal cause is not lost. We are on our way to England, where our own doctor can care for you, and a surgeon attend your wounds. Do not give up hope, Anthony. Paul and I will do everything for you. The future is bright. We are yours as wife and friend for ever. Hold fast to our strength. Hold fast, Anthony, to our love, our caring, and our regard.'

Anthony held me suddenly in his arms, and I saw his face beseeching mine, with some of his old insouciance and sophistication. I bent and placed my lips upon his own.

Anthony died in the arms of Paul, for I was too overcome any longer to support him. I slumped to the deck of the barge, overwhelmed with emotion and sorrow. Our mission had had a tragic end, and one, in some ways, from which we should never recover. I closed Anthony's brilliant eyes with a trembling hand.

We covered the body of Anthony, as the barge moved steadily down the Seine, towards the open seas. And there, at the mouth of the river, a supply vessel was waiting for us. And the aciduous but redoubtable Captain Vicary helped us to mount into *The Osprey*. The body of Anthony was carried reverently below.

And so we left French waters, and headed back to England. Yet both Paul and I were so overcome by events, that we could not approach one another, or offer one another any comfort. We stayed apart, each in our own sorrow. We did not look at one another, and did not speak. We acknowledged only the intensity of our grief and our loss.

CHAPTER TWENTY

I returned to Beaufroy House, and began my period of mourning as a widow, which was compulsory at this time. Paul reported to his barracks, and took up residence in the officers' quarters, there.

Colonel Forsyth came to see me, wishing to hear my own account of events in France. He was good enough to commend me for certain actions; but I found this praise poor consolation indeed for the grief which now engulfed me. I felt that I should never recover again any interest in life, or my zest for the experiences of existence which had formerly possessed me.

Anthony was buried in the private chapel at Beaufroy House. Paul and I were the chief mourners; but again, we scarcely spoke to one another, and proffered no consolation or encouragement. It seemed that the spell of the last tragic events in France had totally separated, and had driven us apart.

To my great surprise, I found that Paul was now Anthony's heir, to both titles, the lands and the monetary endowments, after a generous annuity to myself had been paid. I realized suddenly, that I was a guest only Beaufroy House, and that soon I must depart.

Paul came to see me one day, and I knew he

was attempting to break the stalemate between us. He said, 'I wish to visit Guissley Manor, and to view the house, and gardens there. I wonder if you would accompany me, to give me your advice upon all that will be required to make it habitable, once more.'

And so, in a carriage from the Beaufroy House stables, we set off for this drive into the country. It was now midsummer, and the passing scene was verdant and fresh. I felt some faint stirrings of joy and anticipation to be away from Beaufroy House. The sun shone; the sky was wide over us, wool-white, sea-blue. It seemed that at last my heart was coming alive again.

I had never visited Guissley Manor before, though I had been threatened with exile there, earlier in my marriage to Anthony. I was unprepared for its charm and appeal. Somehow, it struck a chord within me, and I responded to this historic place which had been built during the reign of Queen Anne.

It was gabled and built of weathered bricks; the windows were mullioned, the drives were curved and led to a giant front door studded with ornamental brasses. The gardens lay rather neglected, yet of great potential for improvement. There were foreign shrubs, ancient elms, clumps of unpretentious, almost wild flowers. Again, my frozen feelings seemed to thaw; and I thought this beautiful old manor seemed to welcome me into its embrace.

We toured the panelled rooms, together. I told Paul of the improvements necessary. At the end of my recital, he took my hand into his own. 'Can we not share this place together, Felicity. Will you not marry me, now that we have allowed the decent and required time to elapse?

'Your period of mourning is over in a month's time. Will you not, at the end of this term, commit yourself to me, and let us become what we have been destined to become, for some time, man and wife?

'I know of your personal grief, and this has matched my own. Yet Anthony himself knew of our love, and would have approved our closer relationship. Indeed, his final words clearly pledged us to one another for all time.

'I believe it was his dearest, final wish that we should marry, and spend our lives together. If we do not do this, we shall betray a charge entrusted to us; and the course he wished for with all his heart.'

I looked at Paul with gratitude and admiration for his speech, which mirrored so clearly my own thoughts. And yet I spoke no word of acceptance or denial. I turned from him, as if I could not bring myself to contemplate the future, or to speak.

A short time after this, I received a visitor at Beaufroy House, whose presence greatly surprised me. Mr Grosz was announced, and bowed to me as he entered the salon.

After his usual pleasantries, he began to speak to me upon the burden of his errand at once. 'My visit concerns your Aunt Diane, Lady Bullough, with whom you stayed during your first months in London, and with whom you made your home before your marriage.

'I regret to inform you that Lady Diane has disappeared. I am anxious to discover her whereabouts, for she has left many debts outstanding, and the creditors are pressing for payment.

'Indeed, so grievous is the situation that the bailiffs have been commissioned, and are ready to take possession of Rivermead House and its contents.

'But before this takes place I would like to ask you, as Lady Diane's nearest relative, to accompany me to Rivermead House to see if we can solve this mystery. Needless to say, I am Lady Diane's legal representative, and have full discretion to act as I think fit in this matter.'

I put some questions to Mr Grosz and elicited from him that Diane had disappeared immediately after the affair of the accusation of my being a traitor. Anthony had visited Rivermead House on this occasion, only to find her absent, I now remembered. It appeared that Diane had not been seen by anyone since that time.

With Mr Grosz's approval, I asked Paul to accompany me to Rivermead House. For truth to tell I did not know what I was to discover there, and I felt I needed his discerning and stalwart presence at my side.

When the three of us entered this once flourishing and busy household, I was at once struck by the chill which hung over everything. Clearly the house had been uninhabited for some time.

And yet it seemed to me that there was a presence in the building. I had the strong sensation that there was someone on the premises. We were not alone. Another person was living there.

While Mr Grosz and Paul toured the upper rooms, seeking some solution to the mystery of this house, some instinct seemed to draw me to the study, and I entered this now closed and shuttered room.

I remembered Sir Toby, for whom I had cared so dearly; and how he had spent many happy hours in this private sanctum, composing his Latin verses for the professor in Oxford. I crossed to his escritoire, and sat before the papers which were still strewn in disarray across the surface of the desk.

I saw at once, that Sir Toby had been composing some poetry, when he had been taken ill. It was true, someone had attempted to hide these verses, amid household bills and private letters. Yet there they were written in his precise handwriting; and correctly set out according to the syntax of this ancient language. In spite of myself I began to read the poetry he had composed, it seemed, so long ago.

Mr Hubbard had taught me Latin; I had had no use for this accomplishment in London, until now. Yet as I scanned the lines before me, I realized that there was something amiss. These were no examples of lyrical poetry; no epics; no sagas; no pieces of satirical verse. These were accurate and well set-out pieces of military information. Here, before me, was detailed intelligence of the Duke of Wellington's activities in London. And the precise whereabouts of his agents, and their commissions on the European continent.

These reports had no doubt then been sent to the bogus professor in Oxford; and from there had been despatched to the French high command. Sir Toby had been the traitor in our midst. It was he who had betrayed us, and had betrayed the British cause.

I sorted through the rest of the papers within the desk carefully, and found that Sir Toby had amassed a great deal of information on military matters while he had been archivist at the Duke of Wellington's headquarters.

He had died, leaving a great deal of matter untransmitted. And Diane had then forwarded this information to Oxford. Not in Latin, but in the unadorned English language. Her notes clearly showed what she had done. And the rough copies of her despatches were there for all to see.

I felt greatly affected by my discovery of this information. Yet I forced myself to press on afresh, and to find what else I could to help solve the mysteries of this house; and particularly of the fate of Diane who had so inexplicably disappeared.

I next found personal information of a startling kind. There were letters from Bath to Leopold Vaes, the Belgian diplomat, revealing that Diane had given birth to a child in that resort, and that the child was of full natural term, and been delivered well and alive.

From the import of these letters, it was clear that Leopold Vaes was the father; and that he had accepted full responsibility for his fatherhood.

The infant, a little boy, had been given to a wet nurse, and had then been taken to Belgium to the home of the diplomat. He was unmarried, a man of means, who had given his son into the care of a housekeeper, who, it was revealed, dearly loved this little child.

Other documents showed the implication of the Belgian diplomat in the espionage. He had been the paymaster to Sir Toby and later Diane, from the French authorities. He had visited the house on occasion, as I well knew, ostensibly to play chess with Sir Toby. He had thus become Diane's lover, even while Sir Toby was alive.

Diane's child had not been Anthony's. But had belonged to the traitorous Belgian. And the final letters showed that Diane had fled to Belgium to be with her lover, after her abortive attempt to have me discredited as a traitor.

From the depths of my concentration, I realized suddenly that Diane was now a widow. I did not doubt but they would marry. Leopold Vaes's clear affection for his son, would ensure Diane's respectability, and a new name, and home.

I was greatly affected by this information, and I got up from the desk, and began to walk through the downstairs rooms of Rivermead House. Paul and Mr Grosz were now in the gardens which led to the Thames, at the back of the house. I was alone, yet not alone. For this other presence in the house seemed to haunt me, and to dog my footsteps at my every move.

I came at last to the rear of the house, to the room which had its private entrance from the garden, and where Anthony and Diane had made their secret love. I opened the door, and went inside.

The *chaise-longue* was there, the furnishing, the rich velvet curtains which had shut out the light. And a figure was there, too. Another human being. I saw it was Bloomingfield who rose from the couch as I entered the room. It was clear that she had not eaten for some time. She was clean and tidy, yet her health was obviously neglected. She needed care and attention. And time.

'Why, Bloomingfield!' I exclaimed

involuntarily. There was no menace in her presence; a great pity filled my mind. 'Why are you here? What has happened?' She swayed unsteadily as she faced me, and tears filled her eyes.

'I could not obtain another situation, after Lady Diane dismissed me. All doors seemed closed to me, then.

'I regretted what I had done to you, ma'am. It was wrong of me to approach you with adverse tidings, and sour and make awry your life.

'You had done me no ill. You too were a victim of Lady Diane, but you are not a victim now.

'I became homeless. And then I returned to Rivermead House to fetch some small possessions I had left there. I found the house empty, and everyone vanished. I recalled the private room where Lady Diane had entertained, and I ... I have lived here, ma'am. There has been no food, but at least I have had shelter.

'But I will go now, of course. I have no option. No doubt you and the other gentleman I have seen in the garden will give me short shrift. Yet I beg you not to inform the police, for I assure you I have done no harm. I have taken shelter but nothing more.'

I do not know how it happened, I was never to know. But it was as if a climacteric stormed within my heart, and my mind was instantly made up.

The sight of Bloomingfield and awareness of her circumstances were a catalyst to a situation which needed solution; the solution overwhelmed me with its rightness, and its necessity at the present time.

All that I had learned this day at Rivermead House propelled me also to the course of action I was now to take. The inevitability of this way forward seized and held me in its grasp. I heard my voice in the room, calm, and firm and without hesitation of any kind.

'Bloomingfield, I am shortly to marry the present Lord Glenivray, who was formerly Lieutenant Paul Lycett. We intend to make our home in the country, at Guissley Manor. This will be our main residence, and Beaufroy House will remain as our town dwelling, to be used solely when we have to visit London on matters of business, or in connection with the royal court.

'We shall need a housekeeper at Guissley Manor. And indeed, we need this lady now to take up residence at this house in the country, and to prepare it for our arrival.

'Will you accept this position? I trust you will, for I would prefer you above any other. And in the meantime, please accompany me back to Beaufroy House, where Mrs Colgate will assist you. You need to recover your health, but I am convinced that once you are strong again, you will find pleasure in your duties, and that you will like both Guissley Manor, and your new life there.'

And so it was decided in a moment of time. I told both Paul and Mr Grosz of my decision, and knew their satisfaction and delight. Mr Grosz, as always, took charge of the legal matters. He said that he would communicate with Diane in Brussels, since we had now found her whereabouts. I did not doubt but that she would sell Rivermead House and pocket the proceeds. But it was now legally hers, and she had that right.

No action was taken against Sir Toby and his name was not disgraced. I knew personally that he had taken the path of treachery only for love of Diane and a wish to provide her with luxury. Leopold Vaes was out of British jurisdiction; he was not heard of again.

As we prepared for our wedding, I consulted Paul upon a matter which had occupied my mind for some time. What had happened to Louisa? Had anything been heard of her, since we had left her at the inn, before I had been arrested by the French authorities? Paul promised to do his best to find out.

The information he discovered was indeed surprising. It appeared that when Louisa had had hysterics, upon my arrest, she had been assisted and cared for by Monsieur Alain Norbert.

The doughty leather merchant had elicited from Louisa much of the truth. He realized the parlousness of her position.

She was frowned on by the French authorities as an aristocrat; she had been suspected of being an English spy. She was indiscreet and wayward; a danger to herself and all she encountered in her life.

She had allowed me to go to prison in her place, taking refuge in screams and tears and wild behaviour. She was scarcely a boon to anyone. But he realized that she was friendless and alone. He offered her temporary accommodation at his home.

Monsieur Norbert had a spacious apartment at Versailles, and there Louisa became a guest, cared for by his housekeeper and a small staff. But now it was found that Louisa's own apartment in Paris had been confiscated by the authorities, and her furniture and possessions removed. She was indeed homeless and penniless, and Monsieur Norbert found that he had a liability upon his hands he had not expected, and did not wish to retain.

Yet at this moment, Paul learned, a change came over Louisa. I do not know whether it was appreciation of what Alain Norbert had done for her; or whether, in calmer circumstances, she regretted much of the havoc wrought both to herself and others by her former mode of life.

But she suddenly became docile, pleasant and amenable. She learned to cook; to sew; to nurse; to shop. Monsieur Norbert described her to everyone as his niece. He did not marry; nor did Louisa. Yet she remained within the shelter of his life and home, secure, and, I was informed, contented and happy.

Paul and I were married in a simple ceremony at the village church of Guissley. All our friends attended, and we found that we had many. The Prince Regent sent his good wishes, and a tantalus of silver and glass. The Duke of Wellington honoured us with a portrait of his horse; a steed called 'Copenhagen'.

And with the ending of the terrible war in Europe, with the winning by the Duke of the Battle of Waterloo, the turning blade in the hearts of both England, France and the other countries on the continent, was withdrawn.

The wound would bleed in all our hearts, for a time. There was no escaping this. But we all prayed that the unity restored to Europe would remain intact for ever. And that the peoples of this continent would remain permanently at peace.

The redoubtable Leonard, about whose masculinity there was no doubt, continued to fulfil his secret duties at the Fréjel Prison, until the gaining of the Battle of Waterloo gave him release. He appeared at our wedding as an honoured guest; a dainty, fashionable little Parisienne at his side.

As for myself, it is difficult to describe the happiness which finally filled my heart following my marriage to Paul. I knew that he too, was blessed with a singular joy in our union. We were seldom apart. For it seemed that each moment was precious to us; and we could not bear that any part of each day should not bestow on us the benisons of our love.

Aunt Rebecca came to share our lives at Guissley Manor, she had her own apartments, and dearly loved the country existence in this part of the world. When our family arrived, she was a doting and loving grandparent; she recovered her health, and lived beside us for many years.

Both Paul and I honoured the memory of Anthony, who had retrieved so much in his life by his final sacrifice. Our eldest son was called Anthony's name; and Anthony's verdant memory added another dimension to our service to one another; and our family love.

Guissley Manor rings now to the sound of youthful footsteps, and children's voices. The sharp blade of personal experience has been withdrawn. But the memory of its keenness adds a deeper intensity to our present joy. Without these memories of the past there could be no immediate happiness; no personal fulfilment, and no eager anticipation of the future to come.

We hope you have enjoyed this Large Print book. Other Chivers Press or G. K. Hall Large Print books are available at your library or directly from the publishers. For more information about current and forthcoming titles, please call or write, without obligation, to:

Chivers Press Limited
Windsor Bridge Road
Bath BA2 3AX
England
Tel. (01225) 335336

OR

G. K. Hall
P.O. Box 159
Thorndike, Maine 04986
USA
Tel. (800) 223–6121 (U.S. & Canada)
In Maine call collect: (207) 948–2962

All our Large Print titles are designed for easy reading, and all our books are made to last.